MARK LAMPRELL

THE FULL RIDICULOUS

ANANSI

First published by The Text Publishing Company Australia 2013

This edition published in 2014 by
House of Anansi Press Inc.
110 Spadina Avenue, Suite 801
Toronto, ON, M5V 2K4
Tel. 416-363-4343
Fax 416-363-1017
www.houseofanansi.com

Distributed in Canada by
HarperCollins Canada Ltd.
1995 Markham Road
Scarborough, ON, M1B 5M8
Toll free tel. 1-800-387-0117

House of Anansi Press is committed to protecting our natural environment. As part of our efforts, the interior of this book is printed on paper that contains 100% post-consumer recycled fibres, is acid-free, and is processed chlorine-free.

18 17 16 15 14   1 2 3 4 5

Library and Archives Canada Cataloguing in Publication

Lamprell, Mark, author
The full ridiculous / Mark Lamprell.

Originally published: Melbourne, Victoria : The Text
Publishing Company, 2013.
Issued in print and electronic formats.
ISBN: 978-1-77089-454-9 (pbk.). ISBN: 978-1-77089-455-6 (html).

I. Title.

PR9619.4.L34F84 2014   823'.92   C2013-907012-5
                        C2013-907013-3

Cover design: W. H. Chong
Typesetting: J & M Typesetting

 Canada Council   Conseil des Arts
for the Arts   du Canada
 ONTARIO ARTS COUNCIL
CONSEIL DES ARTS DE L'ONTARIO

We acknowledge for their financial support of our publishing program the Canada Council for the Arts, the Ontario Arts Council, and the Government of Canada through the Canada Book Fund.

Printed and bound in Canada

 MIX
Paper from
responsible sources
FSC
www.fsc.org   FSC® C004071

for Klay
a love song of sorts, my darling girl.

1

Halfway through a ten-kilometre run, you have yet another premonition that you're hit by a car while jogging so you decide to outwit the fates by changing course, heading *down* Hastings Road instead of *up* it. Rather than risk the usual dash across the intersection, you wait at the pedestrian crossing for a sleek green four-wheel drive to pass on your right. Summer is toppling into autumn but it's still hot and you wipe the sweat from your forehead with the back of your hand. Looking left, you see an old blue sedan approaching and make eye contact with the driver who is lit by a flash of early-morning sun. You stride confidently onto the crossing and almost reach the other side of the road when, out of the corner of your left eye, you see something blue.

The blue sedan.

It's less than a body length away, and it's not stopping.

Time slows, just like in the movies, which is ironic because you work in the movies. Well, not *in* the movies, *around* the movies; you write *about* movies, 'clever' features poking fun at filmmakers who may not be creative geniuses but at least they've had a go which is more than you can say for some joggers

> *which is why you have this self-loathing thing going*
> *which is why you overeat*
> *which makes you overweight*
> *which gives you borderline high blood pressure*
> *which is why you're jogging.*

Milliseconds pass.

The blue car moves closer.

You recall a conversation with a stuntman during the making of the latest Mad Max movie. He's talking about a sequence where he gets run down by one of those reptilian-looking, post-apocalyptic vehicles but you're not really listening because you can hear an actor in the wardrobe tent complaining about his costume. He's not exactly complaining, just fussing about how heavy it is, but in your piece for *Cinema Australasia* you say he's complaining because it adds tension.

This stuntie says the important thing is to go *over* the car when it hits. You go *under*, most likely you get stuck on some sticky-outy bit of the engine, dragged along and de-skinned, then kidney-squishingly, eye-poppingly, brain-squeezingly run over by one or more wheels. You go over, at least you've got a chance if you land right.

You don't know how you remember all this in a

2

millisecond but you do. You even remember the stuntie sensing he doesn't have your full attention so he gives a demonstration, lifting himself off the ground. A little jump just before the vehicle hits.

On the crossing, you are not afraid. You feel not one moment of fear. There is no time for metamorphosis so you perform an act of instantaneous transcendence. You are no longer a person. You have become a living thing with a singular objective: to remain what you are: alive.

You start to turn to face the blue car but you can't turn far in a millisecond. You can *think* a lot but you can't *do* a lot. You do, however, manage to raise yourself off the road a little before the car drives into your left thigh, still in slow motion.

You feel no pain.

And that's all you remember.

Inside the blue sedan, Frannie Prager is running late for work. A traffic jam on the highway has prompted her to take a shortcut and it's the first time she's driven this way by herself although she's done it before with her husband behind the wheel. She's enjoying the leafy road lined with old-money mansions and is mid-fantasy, playing the mistress of one particular Spanish Mission pile, when a break in the trees slashes a stripe of early morning sunlight across her face, blinding her.

Frannie dips her head, fumbles for the sun visor and lowers it.

She feels a thump, like she's hit something.

Her windscreen cracks and shatters.

She screams and hits the brakes as glass showers into her lap.

Through the cobweb hole in the windscreen, she sees a big blond man in a dark T-shirt and joggers flying through the air, away from her. He lands with a thud face down, half in the gutter, half on the small strip of unmown grass at the side of the road.

There is no blood.

He's not moving.

The first thing you feel is a lack of symmetry: one hand on the cold concrete gutter, one hand in the dewy grass. You've landed well—pretty much in a push-up position—and it flashes through your head that your stuntie would be proud of you.

You turn your head out of the grass to take a breath. A man with a mobile phone in his hand is running towards you, shouting. He's telling you to lie still, lie still, I've called an ambulance, an ambulance is coming.

You realise you can't move. You can't move anything except your head. And then you feel this thing you haven't felt as clearly or simply since you were a child. You feel really sorry for you.

You start to cry. You cry like a little boy who's been beaten for something he didn't do. And you're sad. Deeply, purely sad. No adult inner voice insists that you contextualise what you are feeling. Children are starving in Africa. People are exploding in Iraq. Millions are far worse off than you at this moment but none of this enters the orbit of your consciousness. You are utterly occupied with yourself. You are a mewling, puking newborn who has not yet learned that anyone or anything other than itself exists.

Shoes gather around you. That's all you can see because you can't move, you can't fucking move, and you can't turn your fucking fuck fuck fuck head. Black-stockinged calves lower into your view. There is a small ladder, just below the right knee. A woman's hand grasps your right wrist. She tells you she's a doctor and she's taking your pulse. You ask her name. She tells you she is Elizabeth Marks. Doctor Elizabeth Marks. Her voice is kind and smart. You do not ask her whether you will be okay because you are afraid of the answer. She asks your name. 'Michael,' you say. 'Michael O'Dell.'

You continue to cry. You haven't cried for a long time and it's like all the times you should have cried and didn't have been saved up for this single purge. You hear Doctor Elizabeth Marks tell someone there is a child in her car and could they please move the car and keep an eye on the child. Another woman is patting your back. She's saying, 'Poor fella, poor fella,' and you think, *'Indeed.'* Doctor Elizabeth Marks says, 'Gently,' to the woman so she stops patting and starts rubbing.

A pair of men's business shoes asks if they can call anyone. You say, 'My wife,' but then you think how frightened she will be so you say, 'Can I call her?' and try to turn to take the phone. Doctor Elizabeth Marks tells you to stay still. You call out your wife's work number in a weepy voice that you have never heard before and someone puts the ringing phone to your ear.

Lovely Lucy the receptionist answers and you know you must wipe all the panic and tears from your voice when you speak. You can do this because you are a good actor. At university, your best friend wrote a one-man play about an aborted foetus who lives out his whole potential life in the moment of his abortion. You played the foetus and it was a big hit. You might have made a living as an actor if not for the fact that you vomit before you go on stage which is no way to make a living.

Lucy is in a perky mood and raring for a banter. She tells you your wife isn't in yet, it's probably the traffic. Or maybe she's having an affair. You make a reasonable approximation of a laugh and add in your best oh-by-the-way voice that you're okay and not to worry but you've just been run over by a car and you're waiting for the ambulance and could she let your wife know when she sees her. Something in your voice tells Lucy that you're not joking because she is suddenly very serious and tells you she'll track Wendy down immediately.

Wendy Weinstein. That's her name. She hates it, or rather she hates the combination of Wendy with Weinstein. She doesn't mind them separately and she doesn't mind the alliteration. It's the desperation, she says, of the white-bread, Anglo-Protestant Wendy working so hard to apologise for the unequivocally Jewish Weinstein. She could have changed her surname to O'Dell when you got married but she's a feminist and refused to sell either the sisterhood or Judaism short. You weren't going to argue because she's cleverer than you and whenever you argue you lose.

Something pops into your head. The driver. Is the driver of the blue car okay?

'Where's the driver?' you ask Doctor Elizabeth Marks.

'I'm here,' answers a small female voice as a pair of tired brown pumps enters the peripheral vision of your right eye.

You recall the old blue sedan, hear the trace of an accent, mid-European, and construct a picture of your assailant working herself to exhaustion in a tedious, underpaid job she's nonetheless grateful to have and now terrified she'll lose if she arrives late.

'Are you okay?' you ask and then assure her you're going to be okay too.

How do you know this? How do you fucking know this?

You hear sirens approaching. They appear to be coming from all directions and that's because they are. The police arrive to redirect traffic just as two ambulances pull up. You don't see any of this—it's purely soundscape with a running commentary by Doctor Elizabeth Marks.

An Ambo leans down to talk to you and it's the first face you've seen in what seems like ages. Pale brown hair is plastered to his forehead with a combination of sweat and grease. Deep lines that once were dimples are etched either side of his mouth. He asks you questions with stale-smoke breath.

What is your name? What day is it? Do you know what happened?

He tells you he's going to turn you over onto a board and secure you. A brace will be on your neck and it may feel very uncomfortable and he's sorry.

You hear the count…

on three…

one,

two,

three…

and you're flipping over. Knees, thighs, torsos appear.
Then faces, all looking down at you. You can see the sky. A
woman pushes towards you, someone tries to hold her back
but she says, 'I'm his wife.'

And there she is, looming over you. This face you know
better than your own. You read every twitch and flicker, the
slight clouding of her bright blue eyes. She is shocked, shocked
to see you prone; then frightened, fighting the faint quiver
in her bottom lip. Her thick brown-black hair hangs in a
curtain, dangling down at you. She sweeps it behind her ears
and makes a huge effort to look calm, to *be* calm, and now she
looks blurry because there's water in your eyes and it stings
and you realise that once again you're crying salty tears.

They lift you up and a woman from the house across the
road tries to rescue her blanket, which is covering you. The
blanket sticks to the stretcher and she tugs at it (but not hard,
for fear of disturbing you) and says in a self-conscious way,
'Doesn't matter,' and you know she's feeling foolish for fussing
when there are bigger things at stake. Wendy releases the
blanket from the stretcher and returns it to her and you hear
her thanking the woman as they carry you away. And you
carry the kindness of these strangers with you and are moved
by them.

2

You are in an ambulance. The brace on your neck is crushing and claustrophobic but you dare not complain. Your view is restricted to the roof of the vehicle as you race along, siren wailing. You know the route to the hospital and you try to imagine exactly where you are, a Global Tracking Patient.

Wendy follows in her car. You suddenly regret this because you want her with you in case you die. You can't see the Ambo unless he peers directly overhead which only happens once as he checks your vital signs and asks more questions.

What is your name? What day is it? How fast was she going?

How fast was she going? You have no idea so you say, 'No idea,' and he suggests, 'About forty?' and you think, *'Forty! Whose side are you on?'* You can hear, close to your ear, a pen scratching on paper and you realise he's logging all this information and you want to say, 'A lot fucking faster than forty!' But then a huge, horrifying wave of pain emanates from your left thigh.

The Ambo reads your situation and says you can have some morphine when you get to the hospital. This is the first time you are conscious of any pain and instantly you are overwhelmed by it. Unbearable waves ebb and flow over your body.

The ambulance stops and things slam and slide open.

You glide fast down a long corridor.

The ceiling panels are discoloured with age and inter-mittently stained by leakage. Every now and then a panel is missing and you catch glimpses of piping and ancient bits of insulation. It occurs to you that this is how you are going to see the world—through a small window directly above you—for quite a long time.

Countless prostrate patients must have experienced this before you and you make a mental note to share your small epiphany with your architect friend, Felipe: hospitals should be designed around their ceilings because this is what sick people see of them. This suddenly feels like a *really important* idea. You haven't felt such conviction since you had a brilliant flash (when stoned at university) about all mankind saving the Earth from a collision with a giant meteor by travelling to one country so the displaced human mass would make the planet wobble on its axis, which would alter its orbit just enough for the meteor to whizz past into intergalactic oblivion. You can see now that your ceilings epiphany will change the way future hospitals are built and will one day be regarded as another beat in the long, slow pulse of your unfolding genius.

A wave of pain turns into nausea and you think you're going to vomit and you're frightened you will choke on it because you can't move your head.

A bank of fluorescents travels towards you and stops overhead, glaring like a science-fiction sun. You hear Wendy's voice amid the hospital clatter but it's a female police officer who peers over you and asks how it's going.

'Good,' you reply (!).

The policewoman tells you she will come later to take a statement and disappears. Wendy takes her place; she's silhouetted by the alien sun but you can see her eyes are red and puffy. She smiles and says, 'Hi Bubba,' and you say, 'Hi,' and suddenly an Indian doctor takes Wendy's place and introduces herself and you try to hold on to her name but it's complicated and polysyllabic and now it's gone.

She bundles Wendy off to a waiting room and you can feel a prick in your arm and she explains in her rhythmic Hindi accent that she's taking blood and putting a shunt in your arm in case you need a drip and/or meds. Then you hear her drop something and say, softly, 'Oh damn,' and she fusses for a bit and you feel another prick.

She looks into your face and smiles and offers you morphine. You say, 'No,' and explain that you want to be aware, stay in control. It's only a glimmer, the slightest spasm of her facial muscles, but you can tell she thinks you're an idiot. She asks you to move the toes on your left foot.

There is a pause while you try to locate your left foot in your head and send it a message. She asks you to move it again, a little impatiently now, but adds *please* to take the edge off.

'I'm trying,' you say. 'How's that?'

'We'll send you up for X-rays,' she replies and walks away. You feel a lurch in the pit of your stomach.

The curtains slide shut and an efficient voice announces that she's Shirley, your nurse, here to clean you up and she's sorry but she's going to have to cut those clothes off you, she's afraid. You remember that you're still in your jogging gear—dark blue T-shirt and shorts—and are only now aware they are wet with sweat and probably blood.

Underwear.

You realise she's going to cut off your underwear and think,

(a) *I'm wearing the black cotton shorts, a little worn but not too bad*, and

(b) *I don't want Shirley inspecting my cock.*

As if she can mind-read, Shirley places a towel over you and reaches under, cutting down your left side from hip to thigh, then your right. A gentle tug and the whole kit comes away like a disposable diaper and you're so relieved to have held on to this shred of dignity that you don't even notice how she removes your T-shirt.

Your arms keep slipping off the bed as she bathes you and she comments how these silly hospital trolleys are too small for a big man like you. There's something about the way she says 'big man' that tells you she finds you attractive and a number of thoughts form and synthesise into something like this: *That's not very appropriate but it's good if she wants to have sex with you because she'll make sure you're alive aren't we absurd everything comes down to sex in the end even when we're dying does she have a nice body you're pathetic what about Wendy who knew it was possible to feel this much pain surely childbirth couldn't be this bad?* Only in your head, the thoughts don't happen one after the other like they do on paper, they all happen at once; it's like simultaneously watching five different movies but being able to understand everything.

Shirley leans over to shine a light in your eye, providing a brief opportunity to examine her with your remaining, undilated, pupil. She's small-breasted with sad eyes and big teeth. And for some reason you form the opinion that she's a single mother of two high-schoolers which means that you could go back to her place without being disturbed until three o'clock at least.

Frank the Helper arrives to take you up to X-rays. He's hyper-friendly like he knows you're dying and he's trying to fill your last moments with warmth and bonhomie. He rattles and prattles all the way to the lift which whines in a high-pitched, almost human, voice until you arrive with a clunk. Frank pushes you through transparent plastic swing doors and he's so damn jaunty you'd swear he was rolling you into a bar for a beer. His big head bobs and jerks and guffaws and suddenly he's gone.

You are abandoned in a tiny cubicle near the swing doors.

Except for the cosmic hum of the universe, there is no sign of anything anywhere.

You are floating in a pool of pain.

Your heart beats in your head.

Where's Wendy? Why didn't she insist on staying with you? You are going to die alone because she's too polite.

You drift.

You are the drifting.

A huge pale green machine points its blunt nose at you. It hums and tuts and grunts and then nothing. You lie alone until Frank reappears and trundles you back into the lift, through the maze of corridors and out into a different room.

A fresh-faced young woman in a nurse's uniform says, 'Would you like to sit up?'

Without waiting for an answer, she winds the bed up and you can see a nurses' station and other beds and a teenage girl with a drip in her arm sitting cross-legged on a bed, poised over a bucket.

Wendy's compact figure walks towards you. Your mate Dazza once described her (a little too lasciviously for your liking) as 'a tidy ship'. Her symmetrical face is rescued from generic prettiness by the startling blue of her eyes and an overly full lower lip that curves to reveal a crooked bottom tooth when she smiles, which she does now. It's one of those appealing faces that people think they know. Quite often she is accosted by beaming strangers who have mistaken her for a long-lost friend or relative. At the last minute, of course, they realise their error and babble an embarrassed explanation.

Wendy, being Wendy, always defuses the situation with her gracious good humour.

Your wife reaches the bed and takes your hand. She looks like she's been through an ordeal but there's a lightness about her that makes you feel enormously relieved.

Enormously relieved. *Like a million fucking bucks actually.*

The Indian doctor calls you *miracle man* and tells you there are no broken bones; you've fractured some teeth and they have to assess the extent of any internal bleeding blah blah blah and you're looking at Wendy knowing you're going to live and you're going to walk and you're floating on happiness and you start to vomit but nothing comes up.

The dry retching is probably caused by nausea which is probably caused by the pain, your Indian goddess declares in an I-told-you-so tone. Her pager beeps her off to more urgent matters and she orders the fresh-faced nurse to give you some painkillers and a shot of Somethingerol.

You're a big baby when it comes to needles so you feel quite relieved there's already a shunt in your arm. Wendy takes your hand as Fresh Face inserts a needle into the shunt with crisp, slightly theatrical efficiency. She smiles at you but she doesn't see you; she sees the Patient. You realise you're performing in a pageant, the star of which is the Fresh Faced Nurse. You're a bit player, written in to demonstrate what a wonderful carer she is.

You avert your eyes from the needle and notice your left thigh is huge, swollen to twice its normal size.

'It's a *haematoma*,' explains Fresh Face like she invented the word. 'Your thigh muscle is filling with blood.'

You feel woozy.

'There,' she says, as an iciness crawls up the veins in your arm, 'All better!'

But it's not all better at all, at all.

Beads of cold sweat form on your forehead and your mouth dries up. You ask Wendy to get the children; you want to see them. Wendy protests. She doesn't want to frighten them.

Declan is seventeen and in his final year at Mount Karver. He is not a steady student but thanks to his mother's vigilance and his own gift for charming everyone he meets, he's almost over the finish line. Rosie is living in fourteen-year-old hell, teetering on the edge of an eating disorder and permanently plugged into the vicious lyrics of dead rappers. She hates her parents, school and life, in that order.

You know Wendy is in shock and you know her first instinct is to protect the children but you want to shout, 'For fuck's sake! I just want to see my fucking children before I die!' But you don't need to say anything because Wendy knows what you are thinking and takes out her snazzy red phone.

'You can't use that in here!' announces Fresh Face like Wendy's trying to detonate a bomb.

Wendy squeezes your hand and scuttles through the blue swing doors. As you watch her go you remember you're in the same hospital where your father died almost thirty years ago.

You're twelve years old, kneeling in the hospital car park with your big sisters, pumping out Hail Marys, willing Holy

Mary to save your dad. He didn't come to Mass this morning because he was a bit wheezy with the asthma. Mum stayed home to keep an eye on him. Tess, who has just got her licence, drove you and Ingrid to St Agathas.

As Mass is finishing, an altar boy hands a note to Father Bourke. He scans it and asks in his thick Irish brogue that we pray for Bill O'Dell who is critically ill and being taken to hospital. Everyone looks and Ingrid shepherds you outside through a kind of blur. As you get into the car, an ambulance comes wailing past and Tess says, 'That's Dad.'

All that morning and into the afternoon you kneel in the hospital car park as various relatives join your vigil. Uncle Bryan arrives. He's your godfather, not a real uncle, but he's a policeman and always knows what to do. He tells you to keep praying. You pray—harder than you've ever prayed for anything—until the doctor appears, looking tired like they do on television, with his tie loosened around his neck. He doesn't say anything.

You start to cry and Tess says, 'Don't cry.'

Ingrid says, 'Let him cry,' and she folds herself over you and cries too.

You can feel blood leaking out through your organs into the cavities of your body. You try to catch Fresh Face's attention but you're not enough of a person anymore. The pain has frayed your edges until you're barely there. Even when she bustles by and adjusts the flow of the drip, you're unable to reach beyond the fuzziness.

You hear a voice say, 'I feel funny,' and realise it's you.

Fresh Face looks at you and says, 'What kind of funny?'

And now you're in all different places talking to all different people—Wendy, Declan, Rosie, Tess, Dad, Mum, God—having seven separate simultaneous conversations. It's like watching seven different movies again, only they're getting faster and shorter,

becoming fragments

of sentences

words

faces

mouth

eyes

I.

3

Most stories begin long before the point at which we choose to start telling them. You could have begun this story with...

I was born on the green vinyl seat of a two-tone Valiant;

or

I had never heard her utter a single syllable but when Wendy Weinstein spoke, she instantly sounded like home;

or

Wendy and I decided we were too young to have children so we adopted a cat.

But the most useful entry point to the story of your winter that began in summer and lasted one whole year occurs three days before you are run down by Frannie Prager's blue Toyota.

You remember most of that year like you never forget the squeal of nails down a blackboard. Some of it you've had to imagine, darn the holes between the facts to stitch together a proper story. But all of it, hand-on-your-heart, is the truest version you can offer. The full ridiculous.

It begins at Rosie's school, where you are attending an information evening for the French tour. At the end of the year, Rosie and a group of her classmates will travel to Paris where they will practise and improve *leur Français*. Rosie's school, Boomerang, is an institution from an era when people said *gosh* and *gracious* instead of *shit* and *fuck;* it reminds you of jolly adventures in a *Girl's Own Annual*. You can't afford it, but you and Wendy have taken out a second mortgage which the bank thinks is for home improvements but is actually to pay for school fees while you take a year off, researching and writing a book on Australian cinema.

Wendy works as the sales and marketing manager of a company that imports and exports high-end furnishing fabrics. She started as a part-timer when the kids were little and the flexible conditions meant she could pick Rosie up from pre-school or duck off when Declan got an award in assembly for Sitting Up Nicely When Mrs Donlan Is Speaking. With a degree in politics and history and a post-graduate diploma in conflict resolution, she only intended it to be temporary but quickly became indispensable and over a decade later she's still there. The job is neither particularly well paid nor challenging (although the conflict-resolution training does come in handy wrangling flighty designers and belligerent sales reps). Wendy is prepared to ignore the drawbacks, at least while your children are at school, as long as it remains a family-tolerant corporate environment.

Her wage covers your mortgage and some living expenses but, because you are no longer on a salary, a black hole of debt widens before you. Your life savings are gone, courtesy of a sad little high-risk share portfolio masticated by the GFC, but you're not too worried because your book is going to be a success and soon there will be champagne for everybody. Actually you're not that dumb—you know this book might not make you rich—but if it's successful there will be at least two more books: one on Russian cinema and one on German cinema. Eventually you plan a complete anthology of world cinema. You may be getting ahead of yourself but your gut tells you you're going to be okay financially and sometimes you just have to listen to your gut, don't you?

Don't you?

Rosie's trip to France is an expense you don't need but it's part of the deal at a school like Boomerang. Anyway, it's almost a year away, which means you can hold it out like a carrot to coax her through the next few terms without any major disasters. Thus far, touch wood, this appears to be working.

Miss (not Ms) Crowden Clark (no hyphen), the French mistress, approaches the podium and gives the microphone a timid tap. Breathless with excitement, she welcomes the parents and expresses her joy at seeing such a fine turnout. You can tell it's going to be a long night. You shift in your seat and stifle a yawn. Rosie leans over and whispers, 'If you think this is boring, you should try her French classes.' You share a smile and Rosie's boyfriend, Juan, leans forward to catch what he's missing out on.

Juan is living under your house in the single garage you converted into a rumpus room. He's been kicked out of his own three-storey home, one floor of which was designed exclusively for him and his older sister. His parents adopted them both out of an orphanage in Buenos Aires when they were toddlers. Of African–Spanish lineage, Juan is handsome and dark and always being stopped by the police—a living echo of the dead rappers Rosie listens to so devotedly.

Your friends say you're crazy letting him stay but he's been nothing but polite and helpful and, while he remains so, he's welcome. Your friends say they're having sex and you know they could be but you believe Rosie when she says she's going to wait until she's sixteen, which is a bridge you'll cross when you come to it. Your friends say she's lying but it is not in her nature to lie. She may be wilful and defiant but she has always been alarmingly truthful—

Look Daddy, I'm flying out of the treehouse.

I'm just cutting Barbie's legs to fit her in the box.

I'm only using petrol to light the fire.

Your niece Mel, who is thirteen years older than Rosie, says she's the only child she has ever seen advance on an advancing adult; as you stride towards the three-year-old with your finger raised, she strides towards you, outraged that you would address her in such an impertinent manner. Once, when she was four, you smacked her for trying to cut off the cat's tail and she followed you around for days showing you the red mark on her leg long after it had faded, repeating, 'Look. Look what you done.'

While Miss Crowden Clark meanders into a monologue

on the French roots of English words, you look around the restless prison of her audience hoping that someone has remembered to bring their poison darts. Rosie puts her hand up.

'Yes, Rosie?'

'Um, Miss, Ursula O'Brien hasn't put her name down or anything but she was wondering if it's too late to come.'

Later, in the car on the way home, you ask Rosie if this was a genuine question or a clever ploy to end Miss Crowden Clark's ramblings. She rolls her adolescent eyes and looks out the window. You remember Wendy's edict that driving is one of the few times you can dialogue with teenagers because they're stuck in the car with you so you make a few stabs at conversation before Rosie snaps the radio on. Juan shrugs and grins at you in the rear-vision mirror and you doof-doof home.

And that's it. An unremarkable evening appears to end uneventfully. Only it doesn't. The evening may have ended but events have just begun. Something is happening. Rosie's question to Miss Crowden Clark is setting off a chain reaction that will devastate you all.

4

At four in the morning of the day you are run down by Frannie Prager's blue Toyota, the phone rings and you wake up thinking someone is dead but it's your publisher calling from London. He's just touched base with some key foreign publishers and is a little disturbed by the lack of interest in *The Decline of Australian Cinema*.

'Last year they would have gobbled it up, darling.' Your publisher, Maxx with a double x, is not gay but he calls you darling.

You try to sound light-hearted and say that the decline in Australian cinema has probably triggered a decline of interest in Australian cinema, which would account for a decline of interest in the decline of Australian cinema. Maxx chortles and you tell him not to panic yet and he goes off to a banquet.

You hang up and panic.

Maxx has paid you a small advance for the book and you're counting on the next payment which is due on delivery in three weeks. Maxx has called to warn you that unless he makes some international sales he cannot pay the next instalment. He doesn't actually say this, of course; he doesn't need to because this is the subtext of your exchange. International sales are crucial to the viability of this book. And if he can't sell this book, you can kiss the rest of the anthology goodbye. You know this and Maxx knows you know.

You pace around the house and boil water for coffee but you make green tea because it's better for your blood pressure. You sip tea as the sun rises over the Sullivans' house across the road and think *fuuuck*. You look around the house for something useful to do—work? laundry? dishwasher?—but you soon spiral into a financial funk. You're already skating on papery ice; Wendy has mooted the idea of a third mortgage. *Is such a thing even possible?* you wonder. It's your own stupid fault but you were going insane at the paper, writing articles designed to show off your intellectual prowess rather than illuminate the films you were supposed to be reviewing.

It all came to a head last Easter when a young director confronted you during a family dinner at a local Chinese restaurant.

Sobbing with rage and hatred, this guy accuses you of ruining his career and his life for the sake of a few laughs at his expense. As his embarrassed friends drag him outside, he spews this invective of abuse and you pretend you think it's funny.

Only you don't think it's funny.

You go home and spend the rest of the long weekend in bed with a bottle of vodka and eleven packets of kettle-fried potato chips. Wendy sits on the bed and says, 'What are you going to do?' You smash your antique bedside lamp into the wall and Wendy's voice turns icy. 'What else are you going to do?'

Over the next few days you formulate the idea of a book. A whole anthology of books. They will be your redemption, a pathway out of the cynicism. Bless me, Father, for I have sinned and for my penance I will write a beautiful anthology, a truly illuminating anthology, a celebration of the splendid cinematic blah blah blah blah. Fuck that. It's got to be honest. It's got to confront the way culture has been sidelined across the globe while we all cheer madly for economic prosperity. Fuck that. It's got to be readable. Fuck that. You've done readable and look where that got you.

In the end, you pitch Maxx a series of coffee-table books with lots of glossy pictures. The first will contain a penetrating analysis of why Australian movie stars are prospering overseas while Australian movies are not. The cherry on the cake, the thing that tips Maxx into the yes camp, is a series of candid photographs of various uber-celebrities in real-life situations. Uber-celebrities in real-life situations will sell just about anything.

Well, not *anything* apparently. *Fuuuck.*

Wendy's alarm goes and you hear her making the first in a series of expeditions to wake the kids. Soon the plumbing is thumping and bumping and the house crackles with cereal and toast and searches for missing bits of school uniform so you leave the dawn fretfulness in a dark corner to be worried over later.

During the night your bitzer dog, Egg, has dragged Wendy's cashmere coat off the sofa and made a nest out of it. Wendy frantically tries to brush away the magnetic hairs as Rosie complains that she has to leave *now*; she's got an early morning tutorial. Wendy normally drops the kids at school on her way to work but you can see she's getting frazzled so you pile Rosie and Declan into your car. (Juan remains asleep downstairs and will not emerge until midday. He's having a 'break' from school and has applied for a job in a barbecue chicken shop.)

Declan, hunched in the back seat, puts a cigarette to his lips and produces a lighter. You shoot him a look via the rearvision mirror but you don't say anything because you don't have the heart for a fight. He pauses defiantly and then puts the cigarette away. Rosie, mercifully, is in a good mood and hums away to her hip-hop with her headphones on. It occurs to you that not so long ago the car would have been filled with excited chatter anticipating the day's events. You yearn for the time when Declan's idea of a high was batting cricket balls to you in the backyard and Rosie could think of nothing more thrilling than somersaulting off your shoulders into the swimming pool. You shake your head and smile at the desperation of your nostalgia. Declan catches you doing this and decides you are laughing at him.

'*What?*' he asks.

You drop Declan at Mount Karver first, then Rosie at

Boomerang. It's still early which means you'll make it home before the traffic peaks. You can go jogging before you settle down to the day's writing. You decide not to worry about the money today. The day is a blank canvas. You are a free man.

5

These are the events as best you can reconstruct them: as Frannie Prager is sliding the key into the ignition of her blue Toyota, you are tightening the laces on your decrepit joggers and Rosie is ducking out of her maths tutorial because she has left her calculator in her locker. She doesn't make it to the locker room because she finds Ursula O'Brien sitting on the worn sandstone steps of the Year 9 home room with her arms drawn around her legs and her face buried in her knees.

Rosie likes a drama as much as any fourteen-year-old girl so she sits next to Ursula and asks what's wrong.

'Nothing,' replies Ursula which, of course, heightens Rosie's interest.

'Tell me.'

'She's such a bitch!'

'Who?'

And out, over an obstacle course of sniffles and sobs, tumbles the story.

When Ursula saw Maddie Peacock this morning, she was on her way to put her name down for the French tour but Maddie told Ursula not to bother because after the meeting the other night when Rosie O'Dell asked if Ursula could come, Eva Pessites' mother told Miss Crowden Clark that if Ursula came then Eva would not be going on the tour. Mrs Pessites considers Ursula not the type of girl she wants her daughter to be associating with.

Until recently, Ursula and Eva were best friends. A murky incident involving a silver photo frame missing from Mrs Pessites' gift shop led to the demise of the relationship. Ursula protested her innocence and everyone except Mrs Pessites suspected Eva Pessites was the real culprit but they were all too intimidated by Eva to say anything.

Eva Pessites looks like a beautiful doll. Tumbling blonde ringlets frame her translucent face; spectacularly long (surgically transplanted?) dark lashes frame languid green eyes; bee-stung lips, grown suspiciously plumper since Year 7, frame gleaming tombstones of teeth. Some say Eva's smile can be seen from space.

The Pessites fortune comes from earth-moving equipment, not Mrs Pessites' gift shop, which she runs for fun. The Pessites donate large sums to Boomerang. The weekly assembly is held in the Pessites Auditorium. Eva Pessites understands the power she holds and up until today no one has questioned it. Not out loud anyway.

Filled with indignation, Rosie confronts Eva in the locker room. She knows better than to go straight for the jugular so she tells Eva how gorgeous her new watch is and adds, like it's an afterthought, in a voice pitched slightly too high, 'How come your mum barred Ursula from the French tour?'

Eva pauses, her eyes narrow. Other girls stop to look at her. She turns back to her locker and takes her time closing it. For a while it seems she has cut Rosie dead, leaving her question adrift in the ether. But Eva is enraged. She flicks a smile at Rosie, 'How the fuck would I know?' she says breezily. 'I'm not my fucking mother, am I?'

Her admiring audience titters and Eva turns and heads out of the locker room.

Rosie calls after her, 'But you could have stopped her.'

Eva stops dead and looks at Rosie like she's inspecting a dog turd. 'So? Who cares?

'I do.'

'You should mind your own business.'

'It is my business.'

'Is not.'

'It is if my friend can't come on the tour.'

'Ursula O'Brien is not your friend.

'Is too.'

'She hates you.'

'No, she hates you, Eva, but that's no reason for her not to come on the tour. Not until your mother stuck her big nose in it.'

Eva is a second-generation Albanian and, although Rosie cannot know this, her mother had a prominent nose before surgery corrected it. Thinking on her feet, Eva decides to misinterpret Rosie's comment as a racist jibe about proboscisly endowed Albanians and go for the outraged immigrant angle. She counters that Rosie is a 'skanky skip' (*skip* meaning someone who is several generations Australian). What Rosie's Irish Catholic and Lithuanian Jewish grandparents would make of all this, no one can say but Rosie is so infuriated by the sudden disintegration of the argument that her synapses explode. 'Piss off, you dumb bitch!' she blurts uninventively.

'Racist slut!' Eva proclaims as she glides away in triumph.

Rosie, slipping further behind in the originality stakes, fires a final projectile at Eva. 'Suck my dick!'

Once again, Eva stops. Once again, she turns. A sea of girls parts, opening a path between Rosie and Eva. 'Why don't you go suck your black boyfriend's cock, slut!'

Some of the girls snigger.

A crimson wave roars into Rosie's head and she charges forward. Eva also charges forward and thrusts her textbooks into Rosie's chest. Rosie lets fly with a great gob of spit which lands with spectacular accuracy in Eva's open mouth. Eva emits a howl of horror and, spitting compulsively, grabs Rosie's ear. Rosie slaps her hand across the side of Eva's head. Eva crumples to the ground, screaming like her legs have been amputated without anaesthetic.

Rosie sees that Eva is already amplifying the extent of her injuries as part of a strategy to have Rosie nailed as the unprovoked perpetrator of this attack. Rosie no longer gives a flying fuck. She draws back her right foot, intent on shutting down Eva's left kidney, just as Mrs Millington comes sailing round the corner in her signature tartan skirt, red cheeks blazing.

6

You wake up. Or not. *Where are you?* Banks of fluorescents swirl overhead. An institution. You are in some kind of institution. You're ill, trapped in a night terror dream. Wake up! *No, you are awake.* Shapes. *People?* Wendy and that doctor, the Indian one, and other doctors. Fresh Face looks frightened. They're staring at you.

You feel like you've died but the Indian doctor tells you that you passed out. You had a little fit and you passed out. It's probably a reaction to having things put in your veins. Some people get it. Not to worry too much. They'll keep an eye on you.

Wendy looks sick. She kisses your hand. You close your eyes.

Who's shouting? Why does there have to be shouting? That Indian girl. *Indira bloody Gandhi.* She wants someone to open their eyes. *You. She wants you to open your eyes.* You don't want to but you open them to shut her up. *Bossy doctor.* Questions. Blah blah questions and you answer blah blah. And you feel…

the feeling…

the feeling of…floating.

You are floating.

You are

You're thirsty. Parched. *Water.* You open your eyes to find Wendy sitting next to you. She smiles. You try to say *water* but your lips stick together. You push your tongue through the sticky stuff on your lips and rub it back and forth. Your lips are sore. *So sore.*

'Water?' Wendy reaches for a plastic decanter and pours water into a vessel that smells of your childhood lunchbox. She holds it to your lips and you guzzle it like a man who's spent forty days and forty nights in the desert. Some of it goes down the wrong way and you splutter and gurgle, which draws the attention of your Indian doctor. She says she likes your colour and you almost tell her you like hers.

Wendy and the doctor discuss your condition as if you're not there. The doctor feels confident he's going to be fine. It takes a moment to realise that *he* is *you*. *You're* going to be fine. According to her. She even wants you to try walking.

'So soon?' asks Wendy, a little shocked.

'With crutches,' says the doctor.

You sit up and the world seems to drop away from you and

you say, 'Whoa.' Wendy shoots a look at the doctor, who nods and smiles and beckons you forward. You launch yourself upright on one crutch then the other. You lurch forward, a single step on your good leg, and despite the painkillers you feel the horrible throb of your bad leg. Thrusting your awkward crutches before you, you stagger across the cold linoleum floor like a newly hatched stick insect.

'Good,' lies the doctor.

While you're up she hands you a little plastic cylinder and asks for a urine sample but tells you not to lock the toilet door in case you pass out again. You manage to provide her with half a canister of liquid gold without pissing on your fingers, and gratefully make your way back to bed where you flop, exhausted.

You remember the kids again and ask Wendy what's happening with them. She says she couldn't get on to either of them but has left messages at their schools. You know Wendy wouldn't lie to you but it seems odd that she didn't get to speak to one of them at least. Oddly odd. Oddity. Oddingtonoplometry.

A huge horrible wave of pain wakes you but you feel—oddly—rested. *How long have you been here? How many days have passed like this?*

Wendy tells you the accident happened five hours ago. *Five hours. How can that be?* It seems like five months. You've lived through so much, survived so much. You're the discombobulated robot on that old sci-fi show—*this does not compute, this does not compute.*

The doctor says you can go home and you feel like you've jumped from episode three to episode thirty-six. Wendy starts to protest but you stop her because you know if you go home you won't die. People get better at home. People die in hospitals.

A silent orderly wheels you out to the car park but does not stay to help Wendy fold your errant left leg into the car. After three painful attempts, you shoo her off and lower yourself onto the passenger seat. You swing your right leg into the car then use it to lever yourself upwards towards the roof. Writhing maniacally, you manage to bump and drag your aching left leg inside before you collapse back into the seat. You sit there groaning in pain but nonetheless proud of your achievement. You pull the lever at the side of the seat to slide it further back. Unfortunately, it's the wrong lever; the seat-back drops away and you plummet backwards, finding yourself staring at a roof again.

Wendy tries not to laugh. You are upset and angry but simultaneously aware of your responsibility not to take things too seriously given your miraculous escape from death. You lie there for a while, looking at the broken switch on the roof light before you say, 'Well at least things can't get much worse than this.' You will often recall this statement in the year to come and reflect upon your cluelessness.

7

Wendy drives you home from hospital. You feel like you're on drugs. Not the massive doses of painkillers that are coursing through your body but recreational drugs that turn the sky an impossibly vivid blue. Cars wind down the highway ahead of you like a glittering string of jewels. Wendy, driving next to you, smells beautiful, is beauty.

The world is so splendidly splendid you want to gather it in your arms and gobble it all up. You smile. Wendy smiles at your smile. You cannot begin to explain the deep peace you are experiencing so you just blink at her like a sleepy lizard, like a lizard-God. Godlike.

The car crunches into your gravel driveway and you wake. You look up at your little wooden house settled in its untamed garden and feel enormously grateful for the *enoughness* of your life: a partner you still want, children in good health with all their fingers and toes, two cars, three bedrooms, taps with running water.

You just turn on the tap and the water comes! And electricity! And appliances!

How many people get to live like this? You live in the top—what?—ten per cent? of the world's privileged. How fucking lucky is that? How lucky are you!

Dizzy with gratitude, you almost topple backwards so Wendy takes your arm and leads you up the front steps. Egg leaps at you joyfully and you want to hug him but you poke him away from your bad leg with your crutches. The house feels cool and smells uniquely O'Dell—a barely discernible but distinct combination of wet dog, apple-scented washing powder, dirty socks and freshly cut grass.

You stagger down the hall and haul your enormous aching leg into bed. As Wendy fusses in distant rooms, you become aware of other areas of pain, a symphony of minor and major chords playing through your body. You are mega-alert, alive to every note and nuance, things terrible and splendid. And now you are aware of something. You are aware that something is coming.

You are waiting.

What are you waiting for?

An epiphany!

In a flash you realise that there is a grand purpose to being run over by the blue Toyota. You are going to Learn Something. The Universe has a Lesson it wants to teach you. At some point over the next days or weeks, Knowledge will be revealed to you.

You are at the beginning of a Hero Journey. You have been Called to Adventure. And although you have no idea what the journey entails or where it will take you, you feel honoured, thrilled to the core that you have been Chosen.

In your mind you fast-forward to a little café where you sit opposite Frannie Prager, laughing about how unevolved you both were before the fates threw you together and set you on that ridiculous, rocky path to glory those many eons ago.

Rosie bursts through the door and throws her arms around you. Her school uniform smells of stale bread.

'Daddy!' she cries.

'Mind his leg,' says Wendy and you realise she is sitting on the bed next to you and you wonder how long she's been there.

Rosie's distress eases as she sees you are in one piece and her story tumbles out: Mrs Rich, the art teacher, found her and told her you had been hit by a car.

'Found you where?' says Wendy, leaping in from left field.

'At the bus stop,' says Rosie, tackled before she can make her run.

'Why were you at the bus stop?'

'I ran away from school.'

'Why?'

Rosie zigzags through the big beats of the narrative with little regard for traditional story structure. The salient points appear to be these:

(a) Mean mother tries to exclude girl from trip.

(b) Mean daughter supports mean mother.

(c) Rosie outraged.

(d) Rosie confronts mean daughter.

(e) Untoward language employed by both parties.

(f) Rosie accused of racist jibes.

(g) Rosie employs physical violence.

(h) Rosie in deep shit.

The phone rings. No one in your household likes talking on the phone (even Rosie, who rarely engages in the typical adolescent telephonic marathon) but, for some inexplicable reason, Wendy answers it.

It's the headmistress. *Principal* is too benign a word for the woman in charge of an institution like Boomerang. Christina Bowden, however, isn't exactly the scary Margaret Thatcher protégé one might expect. Holding degrees from three European universities, she's an accomplished academic with the aura of someone both absorbed and completed by her vocation.

She tells Wendy she's heard about your accident and apologises for burdening the family with further troubles. She asks if Rosie has briefed you on the day's events. You hear Wendy straining to keep things light, using expressions like 'spirited conflict' and 'colourful vernacular' but Christina Bowden isn't buying it.

She tells Wendy that she is still investigating the incident but that she is shocked by the reports she is receiving. In all her years at Boomerang she has never heard such accounts of physical assault. She reminds Wendy that Boomerang does not tolerate violence, that assault is an expellable offence. She feels it's only fair to warn us that things are not looking good for Rosie. She calls a meeting for the following afternoon but Wendy begs a day's reprieve, citing your lack of mobility.

Wendy hangs up, dumps the handset on the bed next to you and debriefs. Rosie retreats downstairs in floods of tears. You can hear Juan murmuring condolences as Wendy paces the room, white-faced.

'What are we going to do?' she says to the window.

You know exactly what to do. You have all the answers because you are Mr Indestructible. 'Write a letter,' you say. Wendy is the best letter writer this side of the equator. 'I'll help,' you add, knowing she won't need it.

The phone rings again and you answer it because you have all the answers.

'Is Rosie there?' a female voice asks.

'Yes, who can I say is calling?'

Then the person hangs up. Which is irritating because it's rude, and unsettling because the voice belonged to an adult, not a bad-mannered contemporary of Rosie's.

The phone rings again and you scoop it up.

'Is Rosie there?' the woman asks again.

'Yes, who can I say is calling?' you repeat without letting the chill you are feeling enter your voice.

'I'm sorry I hung up before. There was someone on my other line.'

It's Mrs Pessites, Eva's mother, and there's no way you're going to let her speak to Rosie because:

(a) Although you can't prove it, you know she just
    lied to you.

(b) She is already attempting to transgress law 2a of teen conflict resolution—parent addresses parent, child addresses child.

(c) She has already proved herself capable of extreme vindictiveness by having her daughter's ex-best friend excluded from the French tour.

(d) Even in the dim, distant world of daddyhood you have heard of Eva Pessites' mastery of manipulation. She must have learned this from someone, quite possibly her mummy.

You know you are facing a deadly foe at a critical moment. You race through a catalogue of strategies and decide on empathetic engagement followed by unreserved apology.

'You must be feeling very upset,' you say and the floodgates open. Mrs Pessites launches into a tirade on the outrageousness of Rosie's behaviour, peppered with non-sequiturs about the manners of young people these days. It's hard to believe this woman is of your own generation.

You put on your jolly-hockey-sticks voice. Your architect friend, Felipe, once told you that if he met you at a party using this voice, he would think you were a pretentious fuckwit. Nevertheless, you have a hunch that it may make Mrs Pessites feel that you belong to some sort of club that she might wish to join some day and that therefore it would be prudent to behave prudently with you.

You feel your empathy disarming your opponent. Brilliantly, you do not mention the fact that this whole incident is her own stupid fucking fault in the first place. She wanders into this territory of her own accord, offering a précis of the photo frame incident and referring to Ursula O'Brien as a 'girl of low morals'.

A girl of low morals. You tell yourself not to be seduced by the archaic absurdity of this statement; this woman is stupid but not harmless. She is capable of causing great damage.

Damage to Rosie. Who is no position to sustain further damage.

Months earlier, Rosie and the rest of her class took part in a study called *Understanding Body Image Concerns and Eating Problems* run by the psychology department of a local university. You were shocked when the school contacted you because the researchers had felt it necessary to pass on the following report:

Rose Marie O'Dell: elevated scores on scales measuring unhealthy body image concerns and dieting behaviours; elevated scores in measures of negative affect, depression and anxiety; low score on the self-esteem scale indicating poor self-esteem.

Brief but devastating. You knew Rosie wasn't the happiest banana in the bunch but she had a boyfriend and a barbed retort on hand when needed, so you didn't really worry about her. Teenagers are supposed to be miserable, aren't they?

Every week you take Rosie to one of the clinics nominated by the psychology department. After each hour-long session Rosie appears with a pretty young psychologist who smiles bravely and says 'she's doing fine' with no conviction whatsoever.

You've lost your way down this train of thought when you realise there is a pause in the conversation. You're supposed to respond to a pearl from Mrs Pessites but you have no idea

43

what she was rabbiting on about. This pisses her off. So to make sure she has your full attention, she says that her husband wants to report the assault to the police and take out an Apprehended Violence Order against Rosie.

In that instant you channel all your psychic energy down the line, hoping to smite her dead. But it doesn't work; you can hear her breathing. You assure her that Eva is perfectly safe and that Rosie is deeply remorseful. This last bit is, of course, a lie but lying to liars doesn't count. Then you tell her that Rosie is being treated for depression; she is extremely fragile right now, and although that is no excuse for violence, it may partly explain why she behaved inappropriately.

You conclude by begging for mercy. You actually say, 'I beg you to have mercy on Rosie.'

There is a pause before Mrs Pessites answers.

'We're all good Christian people here,' she says.

8

Dear Ms Bowden,

We felt it was important to write to you about this matter concerning our daughter Rose prior to our meeting tomorrow, essentially because there are things we want to say to you that we would prefer not to discuss in front of her.

Firstly, we want to be clear with you that we do not condone violence—physical or verbal—and we believe it is inappropriate and inadequate behaviour, no matter what the context for it. We have had intense discussions with Rose about the use of physical force to resolve conflicts, and she acknowledges that it is unacceptable.

As you know, Rose is depressed and emotionally unstable at the moment, and not always able to employ the intellectual tools she should use in a situation like yesterday's. She is suffering from depression, which began about six months ago and has manifested itself in a variety of behaviours. You may recall that the study on Eating Concerns and Body Image in which she participated late last year alerted us to the fact that her problems were more significant than we had originally thought. She is currently being treated by the St Jude's Hospital Adolescent Unit. We are most grateful for the school's contribution to the effort to help her and we believe that her improvement, in particular her willingness to face and resolve her problems, is directly related to the tremendous support Rose has received from everyone involved in her care at Boomerang.

We are deeply concerned that expulsion will equate in Rose's mind to abandonment, particularly because she perceives that the issues of injustice which underpinned the argument, and which were the provocation for her to act violently, will have gone unnoticed.

Those issues include: the exclusion of another student (Ursula O'Brien) from the French tour because of complaints about her 'moral character' by Mrs Pessites to Miss Crowden Clark (Mrs Pessites confirmed to us that she believes Ursula O'Brien to 'have low morals'); and the racial and sexual nature of Eva Pessites' comment to Rose during the argument that Rose should, 'Go and suck your boyfriend's black c——.' Rose's boyfriend is African-South American. She has encountered a great deal of racial prejudice while going out with him, and is deeply distressed by it. Furthermore, she is disturbed by the implication that she is in an active sexual relationship with this boy, which she is not.

These are issues which Rose feels strongly about, and to which she responded during the argument, albeit highly inappropriately.

These are also the issues that will be raised in court if we need to defend Rose from an application for an Apprehended Violence Order, which Mrs Pessites has indicated she will seek.

We understand that you have a responsibility to ensure a safe environment for all students and that Rose's actions have compromised your ability to provide that guarantee. We promise you that Rose will never again use violence against another student.

We are praying that the compassion and caring which is the reason we chose Boomerang for Rose, and which recently has been so much a part of her healing process, can be offered in response to this situation. We are the desperate parents of a girl in danger. We have always believed that if you give a child enough time and unconditional love, you can get them through anything. However we appear to have lost our way with Rose. We beg you, and the school, not to forsake our girl.

Kind regards,
Wendy Weinstein and Michael O'Dell

9

Two days after the accident, you slide into the chair opposite the headmistress's desk. As your leather belt makes farting noises against the padded vinyl seat, everyone pretends not to have heard it. But you flush with embarrassment anyway. 'That wasn't me,' you want to say, except you realise how pathetic it is to apologise for something you didn't do. You hate yourself for your unmanly coyness.

And even if you did do it, who cares? It's not like you could help it, like you were being intentionally disrespectful. Flatulence doesn't come with an on/off switch. It just comes. Get over it, your internal voice shouts as Wendy hands you back your crutches.

Christina Bowden settles in her leather seat and asks how you are feeling. It takes a moment to realise that she is not privy to the sad details of your inner imbroglio; she is enquiring after your battered body. You can sense a cavalry of pain crashing against the rampart of drugs you have ingested but all you feel is a distant throbbing.

'Thank God for drugs,' you quip.

Wendy smiles a smile at you that says: taking the name of the Lord in vain plus condoning drugs. What do you do for a trifecta, Responsible Father?

Christina Bowden smiles enigmatically. You've been trying to read her intentions for the last hour or so. She's spoken to you and Wendy and Rosie, then Rosie alone, and now it's you and Wendy without Rosie. She's been fair and thorough. She's compiled a report of the incident from the testimony of more than twenty eyewitnesses. A picture of the conflict has emerged that is neither as benign as Rosie's version nor as harrowing as Eva's. Clearly both girls are at fault but as Christina, *call me Christina*, has reminded you twice now, Rosie initiated an assault and assault is an expellable offence. Christina has listened to Rosie's ire about Mrs Pessites' behaviour and Eva's response. She has spoken to Rosie kindly and at length about anger management and the application of emotional intelligence. She has been meticulous in her handling of the whole affair.

And suddenly you realise why. *She's going to expel Rosie.* If she were going to suspend her, this meeting would have been short and sweet. It's obvious that the appropriate response to Rosie's behaviour is a short suspension. But there is no way Christina Bowden can turn her back on the Pessites money. You see now that this woman before you has no choice. It's not that she wants to expel Rosie. She has to. And she has to be seen to be doing it for all the right reasons. This inquiry is a means of convincing everyone—even herself—that justice is being done. But the instant Rosie O'Dell hit Eva Pessites, her fate was sealed.

'Your letter made quite an impression,' begins Christina.

You brace yourself for the systematic dismissal of all of Wendy's finely penned arguments and think *not without a fight, Honey Bunch, you're not getting rid of us that easy.* You shift in your seat and a fabricated fart rips through the room. But this time you're glad. You only wish it came with a smell.

'The letter made an impression, did it?' you ask, edging your disdain with a tint of anger.

Wendy turns, startled by your tone. The headmistress draws herself up in her chair and presses on. 'I took the liberty of sharing it with the deputy and the school board.' Here she pauses for dramatic effect but you're not putting up with any of that shit.

'And?' you say, sounding incredibly bored.

Wendy places her hand on yours. To the casual observer, it would appear she is resting it there as a sign of support and affection but underneath there is a vice-like grip that warns: one more word and I'll snap your fingers off.

Call-me-Christina smiles. 'We all agree that expulsion would be an excessive response to these particular circumstances.'

Rosie is recalled to the room and informed that she will be suspended for two and a half weeks until the holidays. She may resume classes and make a fresh start in the new term.

She sags with relief and her little face crumples into tears. Wendy hugs her and you rub her back as she sobs her gratitude to the headmistress.

10

You have no idea why, but on the way home your robust good humour withers. You feel like the drugs are no longer doing their trick. The rampart corrodes. Pain leaks in through the cracks and fissures. You stagger into bed and sleep. Time becomes liquid. Your mind and body float, absorbed in an orchestration of healing. You wake regularly—every hour or so—because of the Dream.

The Dream—with minor variations—goes like this: you're running down a road, not *the* road, not Hastings Road, just some generic street. The ground cracks open at your feet. Sometimes some kind of furry little marsupial scurries out of the crack. Sometimes it's not a road, it's a forest path, or a beach track, or a city sidewalk. But the ground always cracks open and that's when you leap. Sometimes you leap over the crack and/or marsupial and sometimes you leap backwards, stopping just before you plummet into the abyss.

But you *always* leap, jerking your legs in a reflex that sends hot spurs of pain spearing through your swollen left thigh. You wake in agony, writhing on the bed. After the initial horror, you almost like it. Your waking hours are unequivocally occupied; there is no room in your schedule to angst over your book or panic over your impending financial doom or worry about your children. There is only pain.

Four and a half days after you are run down by Frannie Prager's blue Toyota and two days after the Victory at Boomerang, you wake from the Dream to realise that your sister Tess is sitting in the room. She frowns, says, 'Hello,' and lifts the sweaty fringe of hair plastered onto your forehead. She is right next to you, touching you, but so far away you cannot speak to her. Ingrid's daughter, Mel, hovers in the doorway, frowning. You drift back into the darkness.

Across town, parents and pupils applaud as a burgundy velvet curtain lowers on the Boomerang school choir. The girls have completed another successful annual recital, centre stage of the city's town hall, a late-nineteenth-century sandstone stab at colonial grandeur.

Rosie is not present, of course, because of her suspension. Also because she would 'rather gargle cat vomit than join a choir'. Some of Rosie's friends, however, are choristers and they huddle together to discuss the latest turn of events in the Eva–Rosie scandal. Later they report every detail of the evening to Rosie who reports it to Wendy who tells you.

Eva has made her first appearance since her big ordeal, sitting in the audience looking pale and brave, too weak to applaud with any vigour. The class is divided: half in support of Rosie and half in support of Eva.

Rosie's little gang have discussed it and decided to be nice to Eva, but only to her face. Maddie Peacock has already been on a reconnaissance mission to check out Eva's new diamond pendant ('Hey Eva, hope you're feeling better') and is midway through a report on the number, size and shape of the diamonds when a young man approaches. He is impeccably groomed, with gold skin and floppy hair. The girls recognise him as Eva's sixteen-year-old brother, Perry.

Perry pops his head into the circle of girls as if he has a special secret to share. 'If any of you bitches does anything to my sister, you'll pay. You might be standing on the station and a hand will push you in front of the train. Or waiting at the lights and end up under a truck. Or coming out of the movies and have your brains bashed in. You won't see anyone coming but we'll get you.'

A shaken Ursula O'Brien immediately reports the incident to her parents. Having experienced the full force of the Pessites' displeasure during the photo frame debacle, the O'Briens barely raised a voice in protest over Mrs Pessites' abortive attempt to exclude Ursula from the French tour. Back home over a cup of tea, they convince themselves that appalling Perry is merely making idle threats. They remind Ursula how painful things can get when blown out of proportion. Concluding that the best course of action is to do nothing, they pack Ursula off to bed. She brushes her teeth with her stomach churning, feeling like she wants to cry.

On her way to school, Maddie Peacock waits for the train with her friends. Chatting happily, she notices Eva Pessites standing on the opposite platform, surrounded by her acolytes. Eva is laughing and pointing in Maddie's direction. Maddie looks around to see what the joke is. Then she looks down. She can't believe it. She's wearing her pyjama pants and suddenly everyone on the crowded platform notices. Maddie feels a hand shove her from behind. She stumbles forward, trips over her school bag and tumbles onto the cold steel tracks just as the train roars into the station.

Screaming in terror, Maddie wakes and writhes inconsolably in her stepmother's arms. Maddie had decided to withhold the Perry Pessites story as a punishment for not being allowed to have a Big Mac before the recital, but now it spews out with terrifying velocity.

In the morning, Maddie's stepmother calls Maddie's father, who is on a business trip in New York. Maddie's father briefs his lawyer. The lawyer fires off an email to the school.

The email arrives at 11pm and is opened the next morning by Christina Bowden's devoted secretary, Judy, who prints it out and rushes it to the teachers' lounge wearing her *here's trouble* smile-frown. The headmistress has almost finished a touch-base breakfast with the science teachers when a hard copy of the email slips onto her lap. She scans it, finishes her gently risqué anecdote about frictionless pucks, and re-schedules her morning. By recess she has questioned all the girls involved and by lunch George Pessites is sitting in her office, apoplectic with rage.

How dare they threaten him with legal action when it was his daughter who was beaten up! How dare they!

Christina Bowden allows him to spin around her office like an exploding Catherine wheel. When he is spent, the headmistress explains that the Peacocks are not threatening to sue Mr Pessites—they are threatening to sue the school for failing to protect their daughter from assault.

'But Perry didn't touch them. And anyway he's just sticking up for his sister,' he replies, abandoning rage to experiment with hurt and bewilderment.

Christina is about to launch into an exploration of the ethics of his son's behaviour but thinks better of it. Instead she explains that Perry's threats can indeed be legally interpreted as a form of assault but that, regardless of this, Mr Pessites must see that this atmosphere of hatred and revenge cannot be tolerated in a school professing to embrace Christian values. George Pessites is appropriately chastened by the mention of Our Lord and after inspecting a model of the new gymnasium he heads off, promising to 'lay down the law' to his kids.

On the way home George smiles to himself and says, 'On ya Perry,' to the luxury leather interior of his special edition Porsche, just as a Subaru hatchback stops dead in front of him. He slams on the brakes but it's too late.

As air bags explode around him, George Pessites calculates that his three-hundred-thousand-dollar car will be off the road for at least two weeks. He'll be driving around in some crap loaner all because Christina Bowden called him up to school. All because Perry put some little bitches in their place. All because the little bitches were giving Eva a hard time. All because one little bitch in particular punched his Eva and called her names. What was her name? Ruthie? Rosie?

The tow-truck driver drops George outside a row of expensively renovated neo-Federation shops where Mr Pessites enters his wife's emporium—*All Gifts Great and Small*—to get the keys to her Audi when, as fortune would have it, he meets Constable Lance Johnstone.

Constable Johnstone is tall and thin with once-carrot hair that is fading to a dull brown. He has been a member of the police force for just over ten years. He joined in his late twenties after a number of unsuccessful attempts at various careers in sales. Selling life insurance was a little too esoteric for Lance so he moved on to selling objects—cars, kitchens, appliances—but never found his niche until the store where he was working was held up one day. He got talking to the cop who arrived long after a young man of Middle Eastern appearance absconded with just over a thousand dollars cash and seven laptops, and discovered that he wanted to become a police officer.

Lance signed up, filled with hope and ambition. Finally on the right path, he secretly dreamed that he would be promoted to commissioner in record time. But today, on the wrong side of forty, Lance remains a constable for reasons that elude him. He is a disappointed man who consoles himself with the small compensations that being a member of the police force afford him.

Mrs Pessites never fails to compensate Constable Johnstone

with a twenty-five per cent discount on any of his purchases from *All Gifts Great and Small*. When wrapping his selected gift she often slips in another gift of greater value than the one he has purchased. Today, for example, an eighteen-dollar (marked down from $24.99) pewter mug purchased for his great-nephew's christening has been supplemented with a sterling silver baby rattle normally retailing for $49.99 but included gratis. He knows it's Mrs Pessites' way of thanking him for his service to the public and he is graciously accepting her wrapped-and-ribboned offering when George Pessites walks through the door.

Constable Johnstone almost wets himself. George is very rich and owns lots of really big trucks. For a sweet second the constable is as giddy as a teenager but collects himself and adjusts his gun belt with appropriate gravitas. When George Pessites says, 'Hello Lance,' Lance can't believe that amongst all the important information George carries around in his brain, he has bothered to remember his, Lance's, name. It's quite a compliment and the constable is more than a little chuffed until he remembers that he is wearing a name tag.

After an exchange of pleasantries, George asks Lance to join him for a drink in the pub; there's a matter he'd like to discuss. Lance declines with a gesture that he hopes strikes the perfect balance between respect and firmness, explaining, like it's a unique and saintly attribute, that he never drinks when he's on duty.

George says, 'Then have a lemonade,' and heads out the door, certain that Constable Lance Johnstone is right behind him.

11

Wendy is at work, Declan is at school and Rosie is still at home, talking to Juan downstairs. Listening to the rumble of their voices below, you are slumped at the dining table in front of a cold bowl of uneaten porridge when you remember a doctor's appointment. You are not supposed to drive because you are still on crutches but you can think of no other way to get there so you hobble down to the car.

As you manoeuvre yourself into the old Volvo, it occurs to you that you should really move the appointment to another time when Wendy is available to drive you. Trouble is, it's hard to get an appointment with the good doctor because he's popular because he's a good doctor.

You need to see him because something has started to happen to you, almost on a daily basis: a kind of despair descends and paralyses you, sometimes for an hour or two, sometimes longer. You feel it like a chemical wash emanating from some mysterious point at the top of your head and soaking your brain until you can no longer function.

Mostly you can sleep it off—after an hour or so in bed you wake and are able to carry on—but sometimes it lasts all day until the next morning when you wake feeling slightly disappointed that you are still alive. This cannot continue: you have books to write, a family to support. You have every faith the good doctor will help put things right. *Who knows? It could be something as simple as a vitamin deficiency.*

Fortunately the Volvo is an automatic so you park your swollen left leg to the side and operate the brake and accelerator in the usual way. As you crunch out of the gravel driveway, you're feeling light-headed and a little guilty for driving in such a state but you tell yourself it's only up the hill, and you drive—well, like a Volvo driver—practically crawling all the way to the car park next to the doctor's surgery.

You writhe and hump and hoist yourself out of the car and are attempting to extract your crutches from the back seat when you hear a voice say, 'What happened to you?' You turn to see one of the dads from Boomerang. You can't remember his name but you know he lives nearby. You've spent the odd Saturday morning with him chatting on the sidelines while Rosie and his big-boned blonde daughter play soccer. He's visiting the doctor too so he escorts you inside.

The waiting room is full except for two empty seats so you wedge yourselves in with the snuffling, coughing hordes and throw hateful glances at the reception Nazi who has gleefully informed you that the doctor is running at least half an hour late. What's-his-name asks hushed questions about your accident, which you answer in a voice likewise lowered, as if you're talking in a library. If the point of this is privacy you are wasting your time because everyone in the tiny room can hear you.

Half an hour later the name *Jason* pops into your head. *What's-his-name has a name. Jason.* You mentally raise your fist in a victory salute and proceed to overcompensate by inserting 'Jason' into every sentence you utter. Just as the conversation is flagging, Jason asks how Rosie is going. He does this in a voice so quiet you have to lip-read.

So he knows, you think. *Of course he fucking knows! The whole school knows.*

Jason uses phrases like 'storm in a teacup' to let you know he's on your side. Then he does something oddly intimate: he puts his hand on your forearm and moves in close enough to kiss you. In a tiny whisper of minty breath he says, 'Be careful of those Pessites.'

'What do you mean?' you whisper.

'They can be...vindictive.'

'Vindictive? How? You mean they'd hurt Rosie?'

'Not physically.'

'Then how?'

'They might use their influence...'

'How? With the school? I don't think Christina Bowden can be influenced.'

'No, not the school...'

'Then...?'

'I-I don't know. All I'm saying is, be careful.'

A bewildered-looking woman whom you recognise as one of the other doctors appears and calls Mr Lind. *Lind, that's it.* Jason Lind gets up and heads out. He pauses at the doorway to give you a reassuring nod, leaving you to ruminate for another fifteen minutes before Doctor David Wilson appears with his thatch of prematurely white hair and calls out your name.

Stray hairs from Egg float permanently through the atmosphere of the O'Dell household so when Wendy decides to multitask and paint her nails while stirring bolognese sauce and talking on the phone to her mother, she is unperturbed by the discovery of not one but two dog hairs drying into the pearl pink enamel of her left index finger. She informs her mother of the crisis, hangs up promising to call back, removes the errant hairs and ruined polish, reapplies fresh enamel, stirs the bolognese, and is about to dial her mother's number when the phone rings. She scoops it up and cradles the old-fashioned receiver between her shoulder and her ear, expecting to resume the conversation about her brother's irresponsible attitude towards money, only it's not her mother.

'Can I speak to Rose, please?' The voice is older, male, with a rough edge to it.

'Who can I say is calling?'

'I'd like to speak to Rose O'Dell, please.'

'Yes, this is her mother. Who's calling?'

'Constable Lance Johnstone.'

'Um. Why do you want to speak to Rose?'

'It's regarding an incident at the school.'

'Do you mean the ar... ar...'

'The fight with the other lass.'

'Oh. What do you want to talk about?'

'I'd just like to ask her some questions is all.'

'What kind of questions?'

'About the fight.'

'Why?'

'It's, er, imperative that we ascertain what happened.'

'Um, Constable, you must be aware that Rosie is a minor. I'm happy for you to talk to her but only if I am present.'

'Oh, yes, yes, of course.'

'Do you want me to bring her down to the station?'

'No, no, that won't be necessary.'

'But if you want to talk to her...'

'Look, I've got a bit of a full plate at the moment; I may have to get back to you.'

You wake from an ugly dream, sweaty and dry-mouthed, to find Wendy frowning into the small mirror above the old chest of drawers with the missing knobs. She tells you about her conversation with Constable Lance Johnstone. You tell her about your conversation with Jason Lind. Could the Pessites be behind this? Why did the cop ask to speak to Rosie without identifying himself? Why didn't he follow protocol?

Wendy has an epiphany: there is no Constable Lance Johnstone. Someone pretending to be a cop has called to give you a fright. Quickly she dials the local police station and asks to speak to Constable Johnstone. There is pause. She puts her hand over the receiver, 'Well, there is a Constable Johnstone,' she says.

But is there a *Lance* Johnstone?

Someone comes on the other end of the line. In his unmistakable voice, Constable Lance Johnstone identifies himself. Wendy hangs up.

A panicked discussion ensues. Could he have known who was calling? Could he tell what number was calling? Is it illegal to call someone and hang up? Over the course of the evening, you try to reassure each other that the constable's call was an insignificant event. But you both go to bed that night feeling slightly nauseous.

12

You are in the doctor's office again, trying to distract yourself by reading your medical details on the computer screen while the doctor takes your blood pressure. He's just weighed you to discover you've put on a kilo since your last visit, less than a week ago, and ten kilos in the five weeks since the accident. You tell him you haven't been eating much and he explains that the radical change to your exercise regime may well blah blah blah blah.

You do not want to be here.

He has asked you back because he wants to discuss your blood test results. And because last time he 'wasn't happy' with your blood pressure. You hate the feeling of the black armband as it inflates and constricts the blood flow around your left biceps. You are aware of your pulse beating in your temple and you're pretty sure that all this circulatory self-consciousness is pushing your high blood pressure even higher.

Finally the good doctor exhales a long breath through his nose, removes the stethoscope from his ears and rips the black nylon band from your arm.

'How is it?' you ask.

'Let's try you lying down,' he says, indicating the examination table behind you. You know that this means your blood pressure is high and if you were in any doubt, Doctor Wilson smiles his winning smile at you and adds, 'Try to think of something calming.'

As he takes your blood pressure while you're lying down, you attempt to make a shamanic journey. Once, years ago, when you were on a junket for some movie—a post-modern western—you participated in a workshop with a Native American shaman who taught you how to visualise a safe place and journey towards it until you arrived at a deep sense of peace and tranquillity.

You imagine yourself walking down a beach towards a warm rock pool filled with tropical fish. When you reach the rock pool, you discover a set of stairs leading to a mysterious underground grotto. Light refracts from the clear blue water and plays around the pale stone walls. You begin to descend. You're about half way down when Doctor Wilson suddenly says, 'Okey dokey,' and packs up his equipment.

The good doctor scratches his thatch of hair and looks at you, unsmiling. This is bad because he is always smiling. He tells you that if your blood pressure remains at this level you will require medication. You're busy processing this when he drops another bomb.

The blood tests have not revealed any specific physical reasons for your bouts of depression but there are other areas for concern. You have appeared before this man with half a leg hanging off and he hasn't been worried so it is with some measure of alarm that you ask him what he means by 'areas for concern'.

Your blood sugars are 'all over the shop' which may indicate your pancreas is producing insulin erratically which might explain your weight gain. He shows you a series of red figures on the pathology report that indicate your liver function is not within acceptable norms. He hypothesises you have had internal bleeding—causing damage to your pancreas and liver—that went undetected by the X-rays taken at the hospital.

He talks about further investigation and more tests and you know you should be asking a million questions but all you want to do is curl into a ball and disappear. You shift your attention between the three white hairs growing out of his left nostril and the uncommonly large pores in the skin on the end of his nose. You force yourself to find the pores so compelling that his words wash over you until your time is up.

Wendy is in the waiting room. She looks up from an ancient *Vanity Fair* with such dread that you decide to spare her the news. In the car on the way home you tell her some of the truth: the blood test revealed nothing about your depression. Wendy says she doubted it would anyway and tentatively suggests seeing a psychologist. You surprise her by instantly agreeing and then mercifully her phone rings and she's busy dealing with a work matter until she drops you home. She kisses you on the cheek, still talking on the phone, and heads on to her office. You hobble into the house on your crutches to be greeted by Egg as if you've been curing cancer and negotiating world peace.

You know you should be working on your book but you'd rather stick needles in your eyes so you construct a More Pressing and Important Task. Suddenly it becomes imperative that this very afternoon you learn to walk without your crutches.

You decide to practise walking up and down the hallway where the walls are less than a metre apart which means you can stretch out your hands to steady yourself. You discard your crutches at the entrance to the kitchen and shuffle-clomp towards the bedrooms with your arms pushing against the walls, a perambulating crucifixion.

You make it all the way to Declan's bedroom without incident. You put your hand on his closed bedroom door. The metal tongue of the lock has not fully engaged with the doorjamb, so that when you lean on it, it swings open. You try to steady yourself, clutching at the retreating doorknob, but you plummet to the floor of Declan's room, landing on your swollen left thigh. You roll over, groaning, as the pain buffets your body.

Eventually you formulate a plan to get yourself upright. You muster the will to turn yourself onto your side and that's when you see it: a small length of green garden hose protruding from the brown cotton valance surrounding the underworld of Declan's bed. You flip back the valance to discover the garden hose is inserted at a forty-five degree angle into a large empty soft-drink bottle. You reach out and grab the makeshift bong and sniff the telltale perfume of marijuana. Your heart sinks: your son, at the tender age of seventeen, has a history with this drug.

On his sixteenth birthday, Wendy found Declan sitting on a white plastic chair in the back garden with tears streaming down his face. She asked what was wrong and he said he didn't know. He'd been smoking the occasional joint but you'd both viewed this as a rite-of-passage activity, nothing to be overly concerned about, until experimentation had become habit and you were dealing with a weeping son.

With her usual thoroughness, Wendy researched the effects of heavy dope smoking and the dangers of hydroponically grown marijuana (up to twenty-five times stronger than naturally grown crops) and you both presented her findings to Declan. He agreed not to touch it again. You watched him carefully for a while and a marked improvement in mood and behaviour seemed to indicate that he had, indeed, given up.

And now this.

You drag yourself onto Declan's bed and sit there feeling extremely pissed off; pissed off with yourself because you haven't been more vigilant; pissed off with Declan for not taking care of himself; pissed off with Declan because you have your hands full with Rosie and Constable Johnstone and your own failing body; pissed off with yourself for being pissed off with Declan because he has as much right to your attention as any of those other calamities.

You look around the room and try to think what a normal, high-functioning father would do in these circumstances. You decide not to decide what to do until you have armed yourself with as much information about Declanworld as you possibly can. You institute an intelligence-gathering search, limp-hopping from desk to drawers to cupboards, rifling through hidden secret places in pursuit of you're not sure what exactly. As you do this, you reflect upon how radically your attitude towards your children's privacy has changed.

In their early teens you would never have dreamed of prying in their rooms without their knowledge or consent. You believed that raising trustworthy adults required you to trust them. Their rooms were sanctuaries; private places in which they might reflect and grow. Those were the days when they attended school without monitoring, when they went where they said they were going, when they returned at the time they said they would.

Somewhere, somehow, things have gone awry. A critical shift has occurred: what was once spirited, courageous behaviour—climbing to the highest branch of the tree, swimming out past the breakers—has become unstable and dangerous. And you didn't notice until Rosie was spewing alco-pops in the back of the Volvo and Declan was wriggling through the doggie-door at 3am with pupils dilated to the size of saucers. *On your watch. And you didn't notice until it was too late.*

Is it too late?

At the bottom of Declan's cupboard, you find a shoe-box of memorabilia: frayed blue ribbons from primary school athletics, pale green plastic rosary beads, letters and notes, and a couple of poems penned in Declan's more adult hand.

You read the poems. They are about death and the pointlessness of life. *Does he really feel like this? Or are these usual expressions of adolescent angst?* Your mouth goes dry and you feel slightly nauseous. You set them aside for Wendy to read later because she is more finely tuned to such subtextual subtleties. A strange collision of dread and pain fells you, and you roll onto Declan's bed.

As you lie there staring at his desk, something odd strikes you about the pencil case sitting on the desktop. The zippered pillow of tartan fabric has a line of clear plastic sleeves across its side. Each sleeve holds a black letter printed on a gold card. The letters spell out a name. But they don't spell DECLAN; they spell JAMES B.

James Brentwood is a schoolmate of Declan's and while there's nothing outlandish about the appearance of his pencil case on your son's desk, you can't help wondering why it's there. So you sit up and unzip the case.

It's filled with plastic zip-lock bags, each containing a dozen or so small white pills. You have no idea what kind of drugs these are but you have no doubt they're illegal. And clearly they're not just for personal consumption. You are confronted with unequivocal evidence that your son is a drug dealer. You beat off panic and rage with the stick of a desperate belief: it's not Declan, it's James B.

You are vaguely aware that James B has already had some altercation with the police—something about joyriding in a neighbour's sports car—and so you decide to analyse the evidence before you.

Exhibit A: James B has a history of illegal behaviour and is therefore more likely to be a criminal.

Exhibit B: The pencil case containing the drugs has James's name on it; therefore the drugs most likely belong to him.

Exhibit C: There is no cash in Declan's room and he is always asking to borrow money. If he were a drug dealer, he'd be cashed up.

Exhibit D: It can't be your little bubba boy, the one who still gives you hugs and sometimes calls you Pa with such affection that you can feel your heart expanding.

You decide to embrace the best-case scenario that Declan is, for some idiotic reason, minding the drugs for James.

And then a red mist descends. *Well fuck him. Fuck the both of them. How dare he? How dare they? This is your house and you're not having this shit in your house one second longer. You do not give a rat's about the consequences, you're getting rid of them right now.*

But how? Flush them down the toilet? If you empty all those little plastic bags, you can dispose of the pills but you still have to deal with the bags. Bury them? Yeah, brilliant idea. Plant hard evidence of drug dealing in your own garden. Moron.

And then you remember it's garbage night. In a few short hours, a municipal council truck will extend its mechanical arm and embrace your grey wheelie-bin from the kerb. Emptying the incriminating contents into its vast belly, the truck will speed off, eventually spewing an anonymous jumble of household refuse into a giant dump far, far way.

You're so angry, you don't even notice that you're not using your crutches as you limp outside and down the perilous sandstone steps to the side of the house where you keep the bins. You hurl the pencil case into the trash and slam the lid.

Three hours later, you are in the study with your left leg elevated because your thigh has swollen to twice its normal size again and is aching like buggery. You curse yourself for attempting to abandon your crutches too soon and interpret your incapacity as a sign that you should try to focus on some writing. That's what you are pretending to yourself that you're doing when you hear Declan come home. He calls out, 'Hey,' and goes to his room.

You listen intently for anomalies in the usual soundscape of bumps and thumps, anything to indicate that he has registered the absence of the pencil case. Surely if he'd noticed you'd hear the telltale sounds of a frantic search—drawers groaning, doors creaking, the dull thud of objects piling up on the bed—but there is nothing.

Does this mean he hasn't noticed? Or is he canny enough not to let you know? Should you march-hobble in there and interrogate him? Should you act alone, right here, right now? Or wait for Wendy and plan a strategy? Should you call her at work? Is that fair? Why are you asking yourself all these questions?

You wonder what happened to the old you—the guy who would have known what to do and then done it.

Wendy sits at the kitchen table, bent over with her head between her knees, hyperventilating. You get her a brown paper bag to breathe into and her breathing slows. You have bombarded her with too much information. Wendy is a super-coper but even super-copers stop coping sometimes. You wait until the colour returns to her face and make her a cup of tea. Then you both retire to your bedroom and, in lowered voices, talk.

You agree not to say anything about the drugs until Declan reacts to their absence. You pretend that this is a valid non-confrontational strategy but you are both avoiding the horrible fight,

(a) because neither of you has the stomach for it, and

(b) because a horrible fight might reveal a terrible truth far worse than the Declan-minding-drugs story that you have both decided to embrace.

A voice way, way in the back of your head calls, *'Why don't you find out? Why don't you just confront him?'* But you shush it away as Wendy read-whispers Declan's poems aloud.

Wendy thinks the poems were written during Declan's earlier dope-smoking phase and that they do not necessarily reflect his current state of mind. Nevertheless she decides to investigate by initiating a chat with him. She finds Declan in the living room watching a re-run of *The Simpsons,* with dead eyes and his mouth slightly open, so that he looks as if he's been lobotomised.

Wendy sits casually on the sofa next to him. Suddenly he guffaws at something Homer says. Wendy wisely waits for a commercial break and tries to engage him in conversation. His responses are polite but monosyllabic. She plugs away until the programming resumes and he turns and looks at her. 'Mum, what do you want?'

'I want to know if you're *okay.*'

He looks at her as if she's certifiable. 'Yeeaaah, 'course.'

Wendy sits there for a while watching him watch television. Spying from the kitchen, you can see her deciding whether to have another go at interaction but eventually she sighs, rubs her knees, and retreats. You both head back to the bedroom where Wendy hatches another brilliant plan: a father-son chat.

You explain that you're weirdly fragile; you don't know whether you'd weep or shout at him but either of these reactions would be unhelpful, destructive even. Wendy says she's fragile too and wouldn't it be nice if we could put our kids in the deep freeze until we all felt like dealing with them. You know she's been doing the lion's share since the accident and you know she's only provoking you because she's exhausted too; nevertheless you say, very quietly, 'Fuck you.'

'Your son needs you now, not when you feel like it.'

'I know that, Wendy.'

'He's... he's...'

'I *know.*'

'Well do you know when you're going to be able to do something about it? Michael? When?'

'Right now! I'll go and grab him right now and beat the truth out of him, will I?'

'Just for once, can you not overreact?'

'That's what I'm trying to tell you, I'm a wreck! I'm overreacting!'

'What? Because that woman ran over you? You were overreacting long before that!'

'Oh, fuck off!'

'No, you fuck off!'

Things descend into a slanging match. For two literate people, it's amazing how quickly your lexicon contracts. Rosie hurls open the bedroom door, outraged. 'Juan can hear you!' she hisses, shaming you both into silence.

13

Two days later at three in the afternoon, the phone rings. Normally, of course, you'd just let it ring out but you are grateful for the distraction from your attempt at writing so you answer it.

Constable Lance Johnstone is on the line. He sounds friendly, chatty even, as he explains he's calling about Rosie and that he's already had a brief conversation with Wendy. Your stomach flips and your temperature rises. Trying to sound relaxed, you tell him you are aware of this.

Constable Johnstone wonders whether you would mind bringing Rosie down to the station for a chat. You ask him what he means by a chat. He tells you that he needs to 'wrap things up' and he really can't do this until he hears Rosie's side of the story. He says this like it's a boring but necessary procedure and he just wants to get the whole thing over and done with. You'd like the whole thing over and done with too, so you agree to bring Rosie in when she gets home later that afternoon. You ask how long it will take. 'Hopefully not long at all,' he says lightly.

It's a chilly day but small beads of sweat break out across your forehead. You hang up and tell yourself you are being ridiculous. *He's obviously a perfectly reasonable man, just doing his job. Just doing his job.*

You call Wendy at work and let her know that you've heard from this Constable Johnstone character again. She decides to come home early to drive you and Rosie to the police station. She reminds you that Rosie starts back at school tomorrow and it's important to keep things running smoothly.

An hour later, Rosie stands in the kitchen with a slight frown on her lineless brow. This is the first time she has heard about the police and she's taking the news surprisingly well. After the initial fright, her tough-girl persona kicks in and she tells you that she's actually pleased to be able tell the cops what really happened with that stupid bitch-faced slut. You know she is saying this largely for the benefit of her bemused audience, Juan and Declan, nevertheless, you ask her to confirm that she knows not to use that kind of language when she is at the police station.

'Der,' she says and flounces down to the car.

Wendy takes Rosie's hand as they ascend the concrete steps to the police station. They wait at the top for you to hobble up the disabled access ramp on your crutches and you look up at them: Rosie in her crisp blouse and skirt, trying to look world-weary; Wendy in her crumpled suit, trying not to look world-weary. Finally you reach them. Wendy takes your elbow as a sign of solidarity and the three of you enter the police station together, Team O'Dell.

The reception desk is a long, unmanned Laminex bench. You stand there, waiting. Several police are seated at their desks in the room beyond, but clearly they have more pressing matters to deal with. A young policewoman appears through a rear door, laughing and holding a cup of coffee. She sees you and comes over. Her bright tone is reassuring. You tell her you are here to see Constable Johnstone. She asks if he is expecting you. You say, 'Yes,' and she disappears through the rear door in search of him. Moments later she reappears and tells you to take a seat, he shouldn't be too long.

Team O'Dell retreats to a wooden bench and sits. Rosie looks at you with scared-rabbit eyes so you take her hand and are surprised when she lets you continue to hold it. As Wendy scans the noticeboard, you remember that she is familiar with this particular police station.

Years ago, when the kids were small, Wendy was part of a volunteer program based here and next door at the court-house. Every Tuesday, she would come to support women, victims of domestic violence, who were seeking legal protection from their violent partners. She would sit with the women, listen to their stories and explain how the court procedures would play out. Sometimes she would run interference between the women and their partners who were either begging for forgiveness or threatening retribution. In the two or three years that Wendy was part of the program, she became friendly with a couple of the police and police prosecutors.

Holding Rosie's hand, you hope that some of Wendy's alumni are still here, that one of them will walk through the door, recognise Wendy, and throw their arms around her. You hope that this warm reunion will be witnessed by Constable Lance Johnstone; you hope that Wendy's alumnus will explain to the constable what a remarkable contribution Wendy has made to the community and what a fine family the O'Dells are.

But none of this happens when Constable Lance Johnstone appears and calls you over to the counter. This is the first time you have seen him and you are surprised by his maturity. He appears to be about your age and you wonder why a man in his forties has not graduated past the rank of constable.

After a peremptory greeting, he asks Rosie to join him on the other side of the counter. You start to accompany her but he says no, just Rosie. Wendy pipes up and says a parent needs to accompany her if she's being interviewed. The constable says he's not interviewing her yet; he's taking her into custody.

Custody?

Rosie looks from the cop, to you, to Wendy, panic rising. You and Wendy bombard him with questions and protests. What do you mean, custody? You said it was just a chat! Custody for what? How long? She's fourteen, for God's sake. Do we need a lawyer? Look at her! Why didn't you warn us?

80

Constable Johnstone informs you that Rosie is going to be charged with assault.

Another barrage: Assault? But you haven't heard her side! She's fourteen, for God's sake! How can you charge someone when you've only got one side of the story? We need a lawyer. Can we come back and do this when we've got a lawyer?

Constable Johnstone informs you that he's going to put Rosie into a holding cell while he gets the paperwork in order, then she will be fingerprinted, interviewed and formally charged.

It is absolutely critical that you remain calm and clear-headed but panic and fury collide with your good intentions. Your mind reels. Rosie clings to you, sobbing. The cop peels her away and she looks at you like she can't believe you're letting him do this. You can't believe you're letting him do it either. Wendy is on the phone, calling a lawyer, talk-shouting in a strange, high-pitched wail.

The cop tells you it will all be over quicker if you all just calm down. You watch impotently as he leads your daughter away and locks her in a holding cell at the far end of the room. She wraps her little hands around the bars and looks back at you, her face distorted. Suddenly she recoils and looks at her hands in disbelief. There's blood on the bars and now there's blood on her hands and she holds them out to show you. You can see that she's going to scream but no sound comes out.

Instead, you give voice to her horror and shout in a huge voice, 'For God's sake! For God's sake!' You point at your little girl and now every cop in the police station is looking and they see Rosie and rush towards her.

Wendy walks back through the front doors and you realise she's been outside on her phone. She asks, 'Where's Rosie?' and you explain about the blood and that they have taken her away to wash her hands. You ask when the lawyer is coming.

The lawyer is an acquaintance of Wendy's from her volunteer days. Shelley Mainwaring is an ex-police prosecutor. She knows most of the cops in this precinct but she doesn't know Constable Lance Johnstone; he must be new. Or newish. She tells Wendy that he sounds like a bit of a dickhead and reckons he's just trying to give Rosie a fright.

Shelley's advice is to comply. Go along with this guy, let Rosie give her statement, and make sure you get a copy when she is finished. There's no way this matter will end up in court; if it did it would be thrown out in two seconds. Shelley says she's not coming to the station—that would be a waste of time and money—and to call her tomorrow and debrief.

Rosie reappears in the company of two policewomen and you can see she is struggling to remain composed. She looks so small and vulnerable next to these two taller, armed women. You want to wrap your arms around her and hobble as far away as you can go.

Wendy examines Rosie's hands and cross-examines the cops about the blood. They apologise and explain that there'd been a fight in the cell earlier and they didn't realise there was blood until Rosie discovered it. You know Wendy has gone straight to *AIDS* and you look at Rosie's hands for any signs of cuts or abrasions, but *Thank God they're clear.*

The older policewoman tells you she is now going to fingerprint Rosie. Wendy asks if that's really necessary. The policewoman—*Carol Fossey* it says on her badge—says yes but you can tell she doesn't mean it.

Carol produces a large inkpad, takes the index finger of Rosie's right hand, rolls it across the pad, then presses it onto a document, producing a perfect impression. Rosie does not look up but you can see the humiliation burning across her face. You imagine grabbing Carol's gun and blowing all these fuckers away but this offers little comfort so you try to focus on the mechanics of the fingerprinting.

Ring finger: roll, press.

Pinkie finger: roll, press.

Thumb: roll, press.

Watching your daughter's lovely hands, you are transported back fourteen and a half years.

You're kneeling on the floor in front of Wendy, your jeans soaked in blood and water. The baby's head has crowned and the midwife says, 'Don't push,' but Wendy shouts, 'I can't not push!' and this slippery little creature shoots out and you just manage to catch her in your hands. The umbilical cord is wrapped around her neck and the midwife quickly uncoils it. You look up at Wendy; she's crying and laughing at the same time and you both try to absorb the miracle before you.

The midwife says, 'It's a girl.' Indeed, she is a girl. You scan her body and that's when you notice them and see that Wendy has also noticed them: her hands. Even on this tiny newborn, the hands are remarkable: long delicate fingers, impossibly expressive and elegant.

Wendy says, 'Beautiful hands,' and you nod, too moved to

speak. 'Great for jewellery,' she jokes. And you're nodding and smiling and smiling and you can't stop smiling.

If anything, Rosie's hands have become more beautiful, stronger and more dexterous. But now they're covered in ink so Senior Constable Carol Fossey takes her away to wash them.

When Rosie returns, Constable Lance Johnstone also reappears. He leads all three of you down a short corridor to a windowless, airless room with a desk and three chairs. There is a beat while you all appraise the fact that one of you will have to stand. The constable leaves the room and returns with a fourth chair.

You and Wendy sit either side of Rosie, opposite Constable Johnstone. You look at his stupid, mean, *ordinary* face and it sickens you, the power he has over your girl. He explains that Rosie can either write a statement or make a verbal statement which would be recorded, transcribed, then printed out for her verification. Either version would be signed by her, then witnessed and signed by her parents. He adds that if she makes a verbal statement, he will have to transcribe it himself and then, attempting levity—*how dare he make light of this, the fucker*—he says he's not a very good typist so that could take a while.

Rosie opts for writing a statement herself. Constable Johnstone warns her to make sure her handwriting is nice and clear, otherwise she'll have to revert to the recorded option. She takes the pen in her ink-stained fingers and pauses over a sheet of unlined paper. Rosie looks up and asks where to begin.

All three adults answer her at once, overlapping, offering the same advice: start with when, where and who. Constable Johnstone repeats the information then admonishes you and Wendy because you're not supposed to prompt Rosie. You apologise.

You apologise.

Pathetic loser that you are, you actually apologise to this cunt who is tormenting your daughter. A monstrous rage rises within you. It fills the room until it bursts through the door, a tsunami of hatred, pouring down the corridor, sweeping everyone in its path, dissolving them, writhing and screaming, in agonising acid.

Or something like that.

More than an hour passes as you all sit there in silence— bar the odd grunt or sniff—as Rosie pens her statement in a clear, elegant hand. Eventually the room becomes less threatening, less claustrophobic; normal even. Your palms stop sweating and you relax to the point of boredom. Page after page appears until, just when it feels like she's never going to stop writing, Rosie stops writing.

Constable Johnstone is not a fast reader. It takes him a long time to get through Rosie's six-page statement. Finally he looks up at Rosie and says, 'I don't think you're being very truthful.'

Startled, Rosie replies, 'But that's what happened.'

'I don't think it is.'

'Well it *is*.'

'I think you made some comments about the other girl's race.'

'Her race? What race?'

'Racist comments.'

'I—I didn't, I wouldn't. I'm not a racist.'

'And I think you said some other things that you haven't put here.'

'That's what happened, everything that happened.'

'I think you punched and kicked that girl a lot more than once.'

'I didn't!'

'I think you did.'

'Well, it's not true! If that's what Eva says...'

'It's not just Eva. I have statements.'

'Statements?'

'From witnesses.'

'Witnesses? Who?'

'I can't tell you that!'

As soon as Constable Johnstone raises his voice to Rosie, Wendy takes control of the conversation. He claims to have seven sworn statements swearing that Rosie punched and kicked Eva several times before she was peeled off her. He wants Rosie to amend her statement to include this, otherwise he may be forced to take matters further.

Privately you wonder:

(a) why Rosie's version of events is so different from the other witnesses, and

(b) are there really seven sworn statements from other witnesses?

Sobbing with outrage, Rosie refuses to amend a word of

her statement. She insists she is telling the truth. Constable Johnstone tells her she is being foolish. Rosie's anguish escalates and she says tearfully that he can put her in prison—she's not changing her statement.

You say, 'Enough,' and Wendy says, 'She's not changing the statement.'

Constable Johnstone says, 'Wait here,' and looks at you all like he's leaving to assemble a firing squad.

A half hour goes by while you wait, consoling Rosie and reading through her statement with Wendy. Despite the traumatic circumstances, Rosie has been lucid and concise in her reconstruction of events and they appear to reflect not only what she has previously divulged but also the version established by Christina Bowden's investigation.

Constable Johnstone reappears and tells you that you will need to return next week with Rosie for a formal warning. You ask him to clarify. Does he mean a hearing? Will there be a court hearing? He tells you, like he's doing you a great personal favour, that there will be no hearing; Rosie will be given a caution instead. Wendy asks whether he can give her the caution now so she doesn't have to return. He says no, that it's a formal process, that it will take an hour or so, probably one night next week.

You burst onto the street like you have broken out of prison. You and Wendy envelop Rosie in an embrace as a pretty policewoman passes and smiles at you and you think, *Fuck off and die.*

As you drive home, Rosie withdraws into a traumatised shell.

When you pull into the driveway, Juan and Declan are waiting at the top of the stairs, solemn sentinels. Rosie flies up the stone steps and surprises you by hurling herself into her brother's arms, not her boyfriend's. Juan pats her back as Declan hugs her tight. It's barely a glimmer in the darkness of this ugly night but as you watch your son and daughter cling to each other, you think: *at least we must have done something right.*

That night you lie awake next to Wendy, torturing yourself with all the things you should have said and done in that police station. You are furious with yourself for your failure to protect Rosie, and you are furious with Constable Lance Johnstone for so many things that you think your head is going to explode. You get up and pace around on your crutches, then go back to bed and writhe around in the sheets.

And that's how it goes for the rest of the night, fury, pace, fury, writhe, pace, fury, writhe.

Like a demented Sisyphus, you roll your frustration up the hill of your impotence until you are so profoundly exhausted that you sleep.

Sunlight streams onto your face and wakes you. You blink against it and turn to see Wendy sitting on the bed, buttoning a blouse. The brilliance is not kind to her: there are deep bags under her eyes and worry lines etched across her face. She tries to smile at you but it looks more like a wince and you smile-wince back, feeling almost no connection to her whatsoever. You're like two strangers who have happened to survive the same shipwreck.

*

Rosie appears at the door, headed for the shower. It's supposed to be her first day back at school but neither of you will force her to attend. 'How are you feeling?' asks Wendy.

'I'm going to go.'

'Sure?'

'Gotta start some time,' she shrugs.

In awe of your daughter's resilience, you say, 'I think that's a good decision.'

The doorbell rings and you wonder what fresh horror awaits. Wordlessly, Wendy shuffles off to answer it. Rosie goes to the bathroom. You hear Wendy answering the door. You can tell by her tone that it's someone familiar and unthreatening. Later you will learn it's Declan's mate, James Brentwood.

James B of the pencil case.

14

James Brentwood leaves the house and Declan appears in the kitchen where the rest of the family—even Juan who has now started work at the chicken shop—is preparing for the day. Declan tries to act relaxed, bored even, but you can see something chaotic in his eyes. 'Has anybody seen a pencil case?' he says, offhand. 'It's James's. He left it in my room.'

You study the porridge that you have been pretending to eat and feel Wendy's eyes boring into the top of your head. You don't want to look up because you don't want to give yourself away so you say casually to the porridge, 'Nup.'

Wendy says she hasn't seen it and Rosie responds as if she has no idea what he's talking about, which, of course, she hasn't.

'Are you sure?' presses Declan. As he starts to describe the pencil case, desperation cracks his cool façade. Pretty soon he drops all pretence at flippancy and starts to interrogate Rosie and Juan, who are bewildered by his intensity.

Exhausted by the previous night's events and on edge about her first day back at school, Rosie bursts into tears. Juan tells Declan to back off. Declan accuses Juan of stealing the pencil case. Juan says he's not even at school anymore, why would he want pencils? Declan shouts, 'Give it back!' Rosie wails like a wounded animal and Wendy yells, 'Stop!'

You grab Declan's collar, pull his face close to yours and say, 'Get down to the car now. I'm driving you to school.'

Declan enacts the small miracle that teenagers perform occasionally, and does as he is told. Wendy briefly attempts to stop you driving because of your leg but you tell her you have done it before; you will not be dissuaded.

You march-clomp down to the car and reverse out of the driveway so fast that Declan turns to you, alarmed. You stare back, daring him to utter one word of protest, hoping he'll be dumb enough to complain *because, boy, once a dialogue opens, watch out!*

Who are you angry with? the voice inside your head says, *Your son or that cop? Or yourself? For that piss-weak, kow-towing performance last night?*

Pop.

It happens in an instant. You started the car knowing exactly how to handle your son, what to say and do. But now your certainty bursts and vanishes like a pricked bubble. Your mind races chaotically, playing out various successful and unsuccessful scenarios. You equivocate wildly, wondering how to begin this critical discussion. *What are the basic requirements of this interaction? You need Declan to tell you the who, what, when, where and why of the drugs. You need him to see and acknowledge the error of his ways. You need to discuss punishment and develop a strategy so that it never happens again. Come on too hard and he'll shut right down. It's critical not to operate out of your anger. You must remain clear and calm.*

Clear and calm. Clear and calm. Clear and calm. Clearandcalm. Clearandcalm.

The needle gets stuck in a groove. All the way to the Mount Karver gates, that's all you think, all you *can* think, until you realise that you will probably never in your life feel clear and calm again.

You pull up at the school and Declan says, 'Bye,' and you say, 'Bye,' and that is the extent of your conversation.

Driving home, you say aloud, 'You are pathetic. You are a failure.'

And then something occurs to you with utter certainty: *the good part of your life is over; the bad part has begun.*

Wendy drops Rosie for her first day back at Boomerang but, instead of heading on to her office, she comes home. When you see her car in the driveway you assume she has returned to find out about your discussion with Declan, but you discover that she has news of her own.

When Wendy dropped Rosie at school, there was a tap on the window and the headmistress was standing there, smiling. She wanted to welcome Rosie back to school personally. Rosie responded politely and headed to the locker room.

Wendy then took the opportunity to brief Christina Bowden about the events of the previous evening. Christina was surprised and, although restrained in her expression, clearly appalled.

Wendy inquired why the headmistress had not informed her that the police were taking statements. Christina said she had no knowledge of any inquiry by anyone other than herself. She had had no contact whatsoever with the police about the Rosie–Eva fight. She had never heard of Constable Lance Johnstone.

Wendy asked how an inquiry could have taken place without Christina's knowledge and consent. Christina suggested that the only possible scenario was that the police made inquiries during the holidays while the pupils were at home. Upon further reflection, it seemed extremely unusual that not one single parent of the supposed seven witnesses phoned or inquired about the matter; under such circumstances, she would expect the school to have been flooded with calls.

Sitting at your kitchen table, it is now completely clear to both of you that Constable Lance Johnstone is a liar; there are no sworn statements, except possibly, probably, from Eva Pessites. Your daughter has been the victim of some kind of elaborate favour performed by Constable Johnstone for the Pessites family.

'What should we do?' asks Wendy. You have a flash fantasy of dismembering Constable Lance Johnstone with an axe but instead you suggest that Wendy calls Shelley Mainwaring for advice.

*

Shelley tuts half-heartedly as she listens to the story of the debacle but the thing that shocks Wendy is that Shelley isn't shocked at all. Sure, she says, you can complain to the ombudsman but that will require Rosie reliving the event via a detailed statement or possibly even a hearing. Wendy says, no, she doesn't want Rosie more traumatised than she already is. Shelley assures her that the best thing to do is move on. Sure, the cop was a dickhead but there will always be dickhead cops; the trick is to avoid them, not confront them. In a few days Rosie will receive a brief, formal warning, which will not appear on any permanent police record. After that you can all put the whole horrible affair behind you, says Shelley.

Wendy hangs up feeling uneasy but certain that the best thing to do is let the matter drop. You have a brief discussion about your ethical obligation to report Constable Johnstone but this quickly evaporates when Wendy reminds you that you both have much bigger fish to fry with Declan the Drug King.

Wendy kisses you goodbye and goes to work. Her kiss lingers and you run your finger across your lips, contemplating the perfunctory nature of your communications these days. You try to remember the last time you kissed her passionately, but you can't. You clomp down the hall to the study, pause at the door, scan your chaotic desktop, then keep clomping till you reach your bedroom and flop onto your bed. You curl into a ball and berate yourself for lying there when you should be working on your stupid, fuck-knuckle, wank-o-rama book. Soon, blessedly, you are asleep.

*

You wake to the sound of a key sliding into the front door and drag yourself through a molasses of self-disgust towards the realisation that you have slept the day away. Rubbing your face, you force yourself to sit up and listen.

The sounds of the house reveal all: you hear the fridge door open, milk extracted, the clunk of a glass on the counter-top, the clinking of a spoon as it heaps chocolate-flavoured malt extract into the glass...one...two...three spoonfuls tells you it's Declan. Rosie, a serious chocoholic, always puts more than three spoonfuls in her milk.

Declan has his back to you when you enter the kitchen. You say, 'Hey,' and it irritates you that he doesn't bother to turn around when he says 'Hey.' You try to think of an interesting question but you can't, so you say, 'How was school?' He mutters something and tries to push past you with his chocolate milk so you grab him and make him turn to look at you properly.

Your son has a large cut that stretches down his forehead from his hairline to his right eyebrow. His left eyelid is bruised purple and there is an angry red half-moon under his right eye.

'God, what happened?'

'Nothing.'

'That's not nothing. Sit.' You say firmly, 'Sit down and tell me what happened.'

Declan sits at the kitchen table. He tells you that he got into a fight with James B over the lost pencil case. He says there were drugs in the pencil case that James B had intended to sell. You ask what kind of drugs. 'E,' he answers. He tells you that he had reluctantly agreed to keep them overnight and that James had planned to sell them at the local station the next day.

'To whom?' you ask.

'Kids like us.'

There are four or five schools that use the station as a transportation hub, making it an ideal trading venue.

'Is this a regular thing?'

'No.'

Declan explains that James is saving for a car so he cashed in fifteen hundred dollars' worth of shares he had inherited from a recently deceased grandmother and bought the 'E' from a mate of his older brother. The plan was to sell the tablets, make a one-off profit of eight grand and buy a car.

It sounds stupid enough to be believable. But something about this story bothers you. Actually lots about the story bothers you, but something in particular doesn't make sense.

'Why did James B leave the drugs with you?'

Declan explains that James's mother is 'gay'. Not homosexual gay, bad 'gay'. Apparently Mrs B questions James all the time, asking him where he's going and looking through his stuff. (*Outrageous!*) Apparently James thinks you and Wendy are 'cool'. Apparently this means you're the kind of parents kids can leave their drugs with. For a moment you decide to tell Declan how you disposed of the drugs but you realise that such a declaration will be incendiary and that an explosion is not the outcome you want.

Declan asks if you're going to tell James's parents. You say you haven't decided, you'll discuss it with Mum. Declan looks frantic and starts up a protest but you cut though it.

'Declan!'

Amazingly, Declan stops.

'I want you to promise me that you will never do anything like this ever again.'

Declan looks out the window and nods.

'Look me in the eyes and promise me.'

He turns to you, this son of yours, brimming with fragile potential. 'I promise,' he says.

'Good.'

'And Pa?'

'What?'

'Sorry.'

You get up from the table, wrap your arms around him and, aware of his injuries, hug him gently. 'So you reckon Juan took 'em?' he says.

15

It's a cold day. The two-bar radiator under your desk does its best to warm your feet while you construct a zinging opening sentence for your chapter on Australian cinematographers. You hear Juan leaping up the stairs, two at a time. He pops his head in the study, says, 'My mum's here,' and disappears. You hear the front door close and look into the garden to see Juan walking out the front gate.

The peach and plum trees have lost their leaves but an unruly arrangement of camellias, azaleas and citrus blocks your view of the street. You hear a car door slam and assume it's Juan's mother, whom you have never met.

You can't remember how you gathered this intelligence, but Juan is in regular contact with his mother and sister although he does not communicate with his father at all.

You know that the father is an orthodontist and a successful one, from the description of Juan's waterfront mansion. You assume that the father is the hard-arse responsible for his son's banishment from the family home.

After about five minutes, you realise that Juan has not reappeared with his mother. You have not heard a car drive away so you conclude that they are talking out on the street. You decide to go out and introduce yourself.

Bernadette—that's her name, Juan's mum—is not what you had imagined at all. For some reason you had pictured a tanned blonde with a penchant for faux leopard-skin but the woman shaking your hand has curly brown hair, a slight hunch and dresses like a woman a generation older than herself. With the trace of a Liverpudlian accent (*she sounds like a female John Lennon*), Bernadette thanks you for having Juan stay these last couple of months but you can tell on some level she resents it. Somewhere deep down she sees you as an *enabler*: because you allow Juan to live with you, he is not forced to resolve the conflicts that keep him from returning to his family home. You are prolonging the estrangement between mother and child, part of the problem, not the solution. *You're not the guy in the white hat.*

The second thing that surprises you is her car. The tanned blonde would have been driving something elegant and European, a BMW or an Audi. But parked outside your house is a ten-year-old Ford, resprayed a glittering silver, with fat, freshly blacked tyres and gleaming spoked hubs. It's the kind of hotted-up vehicle you'd see in a collectable-car magazine.

It turns out, of course, that it's not Bernadette's car at

all; it's Juan's. She has just purchased it for him as a gift for agreeing to come home and return to school. This is news to you. It's obviously news to Juan as well. You watch him ping-pong through a range of responses before he settles on a beaming grin and exclaims, 'Thanks!'

Once you would have been privately appalled by the manipulation: *You can't buy good behaviour! What is he learning from this? What are you teaching him?* But you are keenly aware that your own crap performance as a parent leaves you in no position to judge. It's barefaced blackmail but it appears to have done the trick.

'I didn't know you had a licence,' you say.

'I'm only fifteen,' he reminds you.

'He can keep it in the garage till he's old enough,' Bernadette explains.

Yeah, right. Like Juan isn't going to take it for a spin the moment your back is turned.

Bernadette turns to Juan. 'So do we have a deal?'

'Deal,' Juan beams.

'You have to work hard, help around the house.'

Juan nods.

'Okay?'

'Okay.'

'Okay, let's see what Dad says.'

'What do you mean?'

'Well, we'll have to see if he wants you to come home.'

'Doesn't he know?'

'I didn't want to go stirring him up until I knew you wanted to come home.'

100

'What about the car? Does he know about the car?'

At this point you excuse yourself. You can't believe what you are hearing and you don't want to hear anymore. No wonder the poor kid is messed up; he's probably been messed around like this all his life.

You go back to your Australian cinematographers and spend a productive twenty minutes doodling on the spine of your empty diary. You hear the car start up and drive off. Juan does not return.

Hours later you are sitting at the kitchen table eating take-away barbecue chicken and coleslaw with Wendy, Declan and Rosie when there's a commotion at the front door and Egg starts barking. Juan appears, swaying on his feet. He leans against the fridge. 'Can I stay a bit longer?' he says with a slight slur.

Three days pass until it is time to take Rosie back to the police station for her formal warning. You and Wendy hold her hands as you walk through the doors, Team O'Dell once again. Your gut is churning and your mouth goes dry as you announce yourself to the pimple-faced constable at the counter.

You take a seat on the familiar bench but in no time at all an older policewoman introduces herself as Sergeant Lisa Gardner. You're more than a little wary when she invites you to call her Lisa but the friendliness proves to be genuine. She's firm with Rosie but kind, respectful even, and you can feel the relief radiating from your daughter. Lisa emphasises that you can't use physical violence to resolve conflict. She explains that while the police will keep a record of this incident until Rosie is eighteen, she won't actually have a police record.

If she stays out of trouble, that is.

Rosie smiles gratefully. You look across at Wendy and see her slump slightly in her chair. Her face softens. She wilts with relief.

You're almost on top of those damn Australian cinematographers when the phone rings. Determined to forge ahead, you ignore it and keep typing but part of your brain starts obsessing about who it might be and what they might want so you pick up the receiver just as it stops ringing. You sit staring at the silent phone for a while then dial your message service to discover that your publisher, Maxx, has called.

You've explained to Maxx a thousand times that yours is a message bank, not an answering machine; there's no point shouting, 'Pick up! Pick up! I know you're there!' because you can't hear the message as it's being recorded. Maxx, who has an answering machine, cannot seem to grasp the difference and shouts, 'Pick up! Pick up! I know you're there!' There's a pause before he adds, defeated, 'Oh bugger, call me back will you?'

You call back. Maxx uses the cheerful voice he reserves for bad news. 'I'll cut to the chase, shall I?' he says, launching into a rambling explanation so obfuscated by elaborations and sidebars that you're not exactly sure what he's telling you.

'Is this about the next payment for the book?' you ask.

Maxx huffs. 'I just explained that to you. I can't pay it yet.'

You've been expecting this but nonetheless your heart sinks. Keenly aware that desperate is not a good look for a writer, you remain breezy with Maxx until you hang up. Then you smash the phone into the desk top until the back of the handset pops off and the batteries spring out. They roll reproachfully around the study floor.

When you have reassembled the phone you discover a small (and insignificant, you hope) metal spring under your chair. You are contemplating your next move when Rosie arrives home from school. All she says is 'Hi,' but you can tell she is miserable. Juan is not home to distract her and you're glad because it gives you an opportunity to talk to her. You brace yourself for rejection as she prepares her chocolate-malted milk, and indeed Rosie tenses when you open with, 'How's it all going?' but then something within her surrenders and she collapses on a kitchen chair, ready to talk.

Back at school for a couple of weeks now, everyone appears to have heard about Rosie O'Dell's experience with the police. She is festering in a Petri dish of rumours and burns with humiliation through every minute of every class. She feels isolated and alone and wants to be somewhere else.

You put your arms around your daughter and let her ramble through all the minor and major injustices she has been forced to endure. When she is spent, you point out that some of the class may be behind Eva but the rest is behind *her*.

Rosie brightens and admits that a few of her friends have really stuck by her. You tell her that she is the kind of person who inspires true friendship. She smiles and hugs you and heads off to do her homework.

Doctor David Wilson's winning smile wavers slightly as he takes your blood pressure and listens to his stethoscope. Without comment, he taps his keyboard to call up the results of more bloody blood tests. 'So how's the blood pressure?' you ask, slightly irritated that you are being forced to extract this information.

'Still high,' he says, smiling.

'Higher than last time?' you ask.

'Yes.'

'Would that be related to the weight gain?' You catch yourself referring to *the* weight gain rather *your* weight gain, attempting to put some distance between yourself and the fact that you've put on two kilos since your last visit, an overall increase of twelve kilos since the accident.

'I would say that it is undoubtedly related to your weight but as I mentioned last time, I'm afraid you're at the point where—'

'I don't want to take medication,' you interrupt. You remind the good doctor that you have been able to control your blood pressure with exercise and that as soon as you have recovered, you will be able to resume this previously successful strategy.

The doctor winces as if some remote extremity of his body is hurting and informs you:

(a) that your blood pressure is not just high, it's perilously high,

(b) that this requires immediate medication, and

(c) that you will most likely be on this medication
for the rest of your life.

Without pause he swings back to his computer screen and further informs you that, while your liver and kidney functions have shown some improvement, you are insulin-resistant, probably headed for diabetes. The insulin resistance will also require medication, and yes, most likely for the term of your natural life.

Doctor Wilson turns to you and smiles and you want to smash his stupid caring face into the computer screen. Instantly you are ashamed and look at the floor.

Where is all this is coming from?

To your horror, tears spring to your eyes and you fight them back until you are able to look up again, dry-eyed.

'Depression is not a sign of weakness,' the doctor says quietly. 'It's a perfectly normal response to a life-threatening event.' You nod and wind up the consultation as quickly as you can, mortified by your emotional incontinence.

On the way home you pull yourself together and decide not to worry Wendy with these latest developments. Although there is one issue you cannot keep from her: your impending financial doom. If you lived in America you would probably be suing someone—Frannie Prager, or the man who painted the stripes on the crossing, or the company that built the road—for vast amounts of compensation. But this is Australia and those avenues of recompense are not open to you.

That night, as you're watching a re-run of Wendy's

favourite TV show, you mention that Maxx can't make the next payment for the book. In some stupid part of your brain you hope that the television will distract her from this news but all it does is spoil the show. Wendy wilts. You are about to suggest that maybe you should think about selling the house and renting something in the neighbourhood but the impulse dissolves into a metallic taste in your mouth.

Wendy says you can afford one more mortgage payment and that's it. She can make enough money for food and living but not the mortgage as well. 'Maybe I could get a weekend job,' she offers. You know you should be the one with the weekend job so you say, 'No, I'll try to go back to the paper.' There's a long pause and Wendy says, without looking at you, 'Maybe that's for the best.'

Later, in the shower, you feel the weight of failure pressing down on you. It pushes you to the tiled floor where you sit watching the water sheet down the mildewed plastic shower curtain until Wendy knocks on the door and tells you she is going to bed.

'Night,' she calls.

'Night,' you call back.

You and Wendy sit solemnly at the breakfast table as Rosie hovers in front of you, wondering where to begin. She has made you promise not to interrupt her until she has finished what she wants to say. Catastrophes ricochet around your head.

She's pregnant.

She's pregnant and she got AIDS from the prison cells.

She's going to have an AIDS baby.

'I've decided to leave school and get a job. I'm going to start work at the chicken shop with Juan,' says Rosie.

'Is that all?' you blurt.

Quickly concluding that you are going to be of no assistance, Wendy takes control. Assuming Rosie wants to leave school to avoid humiliation, she encourages her to endure the current scrutiny.

'One day, sooner than you think, it will all blow over,' Wendy assures her.

Rosie says yes, she knows this; things won't be horrible forever. 'I just wanna job, make some money.'

You point out that she'll be able to get a better job, a higher paying job, if she finishes school.

'We've always talked about you going to uni,' Wendy adds, 'doing vet science. You've always wanted to be a vet.'

'Maybe later. Right now I just want to make some money.'

'What for?'

'I'd be able to help around here.'

'With what?'

'With money. I could help you with money.'

'We don't need help with money.'

'Yes, you do. I heard you talking last night. You wouldn't have to pay school fees—that would save a lot of money. And I could pay board. I know it's not a lot but every little bit helps, that's what you always say, Mum.'

'Oh darling,' whispers Wendy.

Those damn tears spring to your eyes again so you study the tabletop. Wendy puts her arms around Rosie and thanks her. She explains that it's not Rosie's job to worry about the family finances, that we're going through a bit of a rough patch but we'll be fine. All families go through times like this and she's not to worry. She says this with such loving authority that you almost believe it yourself.

Rosie's hand brushes across the tips of your fingers. 'You okay, Pa?'

You look up at your daughter so filled with love that you think you might burst.

The *Herald* has been through one regime change and two arts editors since you worked there so, although you know every desk and chair, many of the faces are not familiar to you. The new arts editor is a weedy hipster with a carefully coiffed quiff and a rat-tat-tat manner of speaking. Knows your work. Loves your work. Hilarious. Vee funny (he actually says *vee*).

Rat-tat-tat asks you what movies you have seen recently. You falter as you realise that you haven't seen any movies recently. He reframes the question: 'What's the last movie you saw?' You know you should say something impressive like *Citizen Kane* but your mind goes blank. 'Can't remember,' you reply. Fortunately he interprets this as a cryptic analysis of recent cinematic offerings. 'Ha! So know what you mean!'

You nod sagely.

'So,' he says, inviting you with a gesture to state your business.

Artlessly, you get to the point. 'I was wondering if I could have my old job back.'

He swivels in his chair and smacks his lips. 'If only you'd asked me that five months ago!'

Five months ago the guy who replaced you was replaced by a new reviewer, Louisa Orban. Louisa loves movies. She loves it when the lights go down and the cinema falls quiet and she is transported into other times, places, lives, worlds. There is a genuine infectiousness to her reviews that makes people want to see the movies she has seen. Even the bad ones seem to offer an illuminating moment or a thrilling performance. Hers is a new-wave positivism that is completely counter to your seen-it-all-before-and-last-time-it-was-actually-good reviewing style.

You suggest that you could provide some yang to balance Louisa's yin.

'Actually your style is more yin and Lou is more yang,' he says.

'What I meant was—'

'It's just that I'm a Buddhist,' he interrupts.

He pronounces it *Boo-dist* as though he's giving you the password to a secret society and launches into a monologue that features the phrase 'budget cuts'. It's like one of those comic strips in the Sunday papers where the Owner talks to the Dog but all Dog can hear is 'Blah blah blah Rover. Blah blah blah Rover.' All you can hear is 'Blah blah blah budget cut. Budget cut. Budget cut.'

As he walks you to the lifts he repeatedly pats his right fist with his left hand until he suddenly stops dead and you almost walk into him. Omitting all personal pronouns, Rat-tat-tat makes an offer. 'Hope this isn't ridiculous. But happy to look at any freelance stuff. More than happy. Delighted. No guarantees, though, with the budget cuts.'

You're standing in the lift watching the floor numbers light up as you descend when you realise you can't remember whether you thanked him or shook his hand or said goodbye.

Out in the street it's cold and raining and the city is seething with people bearing dark umbrellas. Putting a newspaper over your head, you launch yourself into the stream of soaking humanity and try to make your way to the kerb. A harried young mother rams her stroller into your shin and frowns at you as if it's all your fault. You limp-push your way to a light pole and look across the street. Your mouth dries up and the colour drains from your vision. You slide into the gutter and sit in a puddle, head spinning.

16

You wake. It's been raining on and off for days but the sky has cleared again. The absence of sun through the venetians tells you that the morning has passed. You wonder what day it is and whether anyone is still home. You feel a movement at the end of the bed and reach down to pat Egg but a hand takes yours and a familiar voice says, 'Hey there.' You turn and focus. Your sister Ingrid is there. 'Can I get you anything?'

Wendy has left the heater on to keep you warm but you're overheated. 'Water,' you croak.

'You've got some,' she says and you follow her look to a glass of water sitting on the bedside table. You now remember your other sister Tess bringing it; the sunlight was over her shoulder so it must have been morning.

Ingrid watches as you gulp down the water. You hand

her the empty glass, say 'Thanks,' and close your eyes again. You've been sleeping since your failed meeting at the paper. You don't know why and you don't care.

The light snaps on and you blink yourself awake as Wendy ushers Doctor Wilson into the room. He puts an icy thermometer under one arm and wraps a black Velcro bandage around the other. Pumping up the sphygmomanometer (*hate the device but love the name*), David Wilson smiles his caring smile, and runs a hand through his teeth-white hair. 'I'd like you to see a psychiatrist,' he says.

'I can't afford to see a psychiatrist,' you say.

'You can't afford not to.'

Your doctor thinks you are crazy and this scares the living shit out of you. You toss and turn for the rest of the night, leapfrogging from calamity to catastrophe between feverish dreams. You wake with the rest of the family and are first into the kitchen, preparing breakfast for everyone.

Wendy is palpably relieved to see you up and about. You tell her that you're going to work on the book this morning and may take in a movie after lunch with the intention of bashing out and flogging a freelance review. Wendy is taken aback by your about-face but you can see she has decided to believe you.

Declan flops at the breakfast table, bleary-eyed, which inspires Wendy to suggest that maybe you could help Declan with a school project. He has decided to make a short film as his major assessment piece for drama.

Declan perks up. 'Would you look at the script, Pa?'

'Sure,' you say, feeling a twist of dread in your gut.

When everyone leaves the house you sit down and read Declan's script. It's a black comedy about a thief who holds up a convenience store. Customers in the store begin to critique the thief's hold-up style, offering helpful suggestions on how to be more intimidating. Eventually the thief unravels.

It's pithy, funny and well structured. You are surprised and impressed. Your son has a gift for storytelling and it fills you with pride. And then relief that for once you can engage in an exchange with him that doesn't involve cross-examination or admonishment.

That night you tell Declan how wonderful you think his script is and he whoops with delight. He asks you if you have any criticisms and looks at you in complete disbelief when you say (truthfully) that you don't. It makes you wonder whether you've been too critical in the past.

Wendy joins the discussion and you begin to nut out the details of the shoot. Declan wants to film at the local shopping centre but it flashes through your head that one of the actors will be wielding a gun—albeit a toy gun—and that this may draw unwarranted attention. Your mind races straight to the scenario in which an over-enthusiastic local raises the alarm and an idiot cop ends up shooting the hapless actor holding the gun. It's so ridiculous that you don't verbalise it but you do suggest that Declan might be better off shooting in a more controlled environment, like the school canteen.

School holidays are coming up so he can make use of the facilities during the winter break without being interrupted or interrupting anyone. Declan thinks this is a great idea and goes off to organise actors, costumes and props. Wendy puts her hand on yours and smiles. She asks if you'll go to the shoot to support Declan during filming.

'Of course,' you say, 'of course.'

Egg starts barking and wagging his tail and a moment later Rosie staggers through the door. She's been at an inter-school French seminar and she looks exhausted.

'I want to go to Mount Karver,' she announces.

Mount Karver is co-ed in years 10, 11 and 12. Rosie's name has been on the enrolment list there for years but up until this year she seemed settled at Boomerang.

'Before you say it, it's nothing to do with Eva. And I know I'm supposed to stick it out and everything but it's not that. I just want a change and I really think it would be good to be with boys as well—good to get away from the whole all-girl thing. Girls can be so bitchy...'

Rosie's face crumples and tears tumble down her cheeks. Defiant, she wipes them away and is about to launch further arguments when Wendy promises to look into it.

You're sitting in a delicious pool of sunlight outside the Mount Karver canteen, reading a book. Inside, Declan and his crew are filming the robbery script. You're supposed to stop any potential intruders but because it's school holidays there are very few people around. Declan calls, 'Action,' and the actor playing the robber shouts, 'This is a stick-up! Hands in the air!' There is the rumble of voices, some indecipherable yelling, then Declan calls, 'Cut.'

You are proud of your son. You know he is going to

make a fine film. You feel this green-shooted thing breaking through the shell of your despair. It startles you with its freshness, this hope, this happiness.

What you don't know is that less than a hundred metres away, Liesel Ham is drying her squirming four-year-old son, Arthur, with a towel. During the holidays, Mount Karver runs swimming lessons in its indoor pool complex and Arthur has just completed twenty minutes of excellent dog-paddling. Liesel pulls a T-shirt over Arthur's wet red head while her two-year-old daughter, Bella, clings to her leg, grizzling. Bella needs a nap and Liesel goes into packing-up mode so she can get her home to bed before the man comes to fix her dishwasher.

Liesel slings her bags over one shoulder, scoops Bella onto her hip and tugs Arthur behind her. They hurry down the path leading to the main drive and, even though no one is about, Liesel makes a point (for Arthur's benefit) of stopping to look left, right, then left again because you're never too young to learn the principles of road safety.

When Liesel looks left the second time she sees something odd: twenty metres away, a blond man is sitting outside the canteen as if he's guarding something; it's not exactly a sinister vision but for some reason it makes her feel uneasy.

Then Liesel hears shouting. 'This is a stick-up! Hands in the air!' Her blood runs cold. She scoops Arthur onto her other hip and sprints towards the street where her car is parked.

You glance up, see a woman hurrying out the school gates

with her kids, and think nothing of it.

Frantic and fumbling, Liesel unlocks the car, clips the kids into their seats, leaps into the driver's seat and locks the door. Checking to see that no one has followed her, she extracts a mobile phone from her bag and dials the police.

The sun has shifted and you're almost in shadow. Feeling the winter chill, you're about to go to the Volvo for your blue coat when you hear sirens in the distance and wonder whether they belong to police, ambulance or firemen. You don't take much notice as the sirens wail closer. You don't take much notice until they are right outside the school, and then you look up from your book, expecting to see the flashing lights whizz past the main gates.

Only they don't.

The blue flashing lights of two police cars swing into the Mount Karver gates and scream down the driveway towards you. You're barely forming a *what-the-heck* when they stop outside the canteen. And suddenly, in an explosion of cerebral activity, a million pennies drop at once. Your worst nightmare has come true: *some idiot has heard the yelling and called the cops.*

You get to your feet, ready to launch into an explanation when cop-car doors burst open and a cop charges at you. 'Stop where you are! Put your hands in the air!'

You are astonished to see the cop going for his gun so you drop your book and thrust your hands into the air. You lift you eyes from his gun holster to his face. Your worst nightmare just got worse.

116

You cannot believe it.

You can't fucking believe it.

Striding towards you with his hand on his holster is Constable Lance Johnstone. *Cuntstable. Lance. Fucking. Johnstone.*

You're a character trapped in a Kafka novel. Or from some B-grade movie. If you were reviewing this movie, you would be pouring vitriol over this improbable plot point. 'Ludicrous,' you would write, 'a ludicrous deus ex machina pressing beyond the bounds of all believability.'

But this isn't a movie. This is life. Your life. Where, you are learning, lightning does indeed strike twice.

Still with your hands in the air you start to babble: a short film. Not a robbery. Son attends school. Son doing drama assignment.

A gaggle of faces appears behind you—Declan, actors, crew members—drawn by the sirens.

Even Lance Johnstone can see that you are telling the truth. He still hasn't recognised you, and you're hoping that he may see the funny side of things and just go back to the station.

Stupid you.

Lance demands to know who's in charge and you say you are. He asks if there's a gun involved. You say not a real gun—just a toy. He asks to see it.

Toby, the young actor playing the robber, produces the gun and goes to hand it to the constable, inadvertently pointing it at him. The constable practically slaps the gun out of Toby's hand and it drops to the ground.

Lance Johnstone reels back, regarding the shiny pistol with horror. 'I would have shot the boy I saw holding that gun!' he proclaims.

Lying on the ground, the gun does indeed look real but Declan assures him that it's a BB gun, capable of shooting only potato pellets. Constable Johnstone will not be placated. 'I would have shot the boy I saw holding that gun!' he repeats.

He raves at you about more squad cars coming, a helicopter on the way. He tells you how stupid and foolhardy you are not to inform the local police when undertaking an activity involving dangerous firearms.

Lance Johnstone seems to be on some kind of loop, repeating the same accusations and warnings, in the same order, over and over again. You can see the cast and crew exchanging glances; clearly this guy is insane. Fortunately they sense the clear and present danger in his special brand of nuttiness and not one of them comes out with a quip or retort that might send him spinning out of control.

The second squad car executes a U-turn and exits the school gates.

You're starting to wonder if Constable Johnstone is ever going to stop raving at you when the young policewoman who has been hovering in the background gently suggests they take some names and details.

While Constable Pamela Bird scribbles everyone's names into a small spiral-bound notepad, Constable Johnstone takes the potato-firing weapon to his car. He tells Pam he has to make urgent radio calls to halt the legions of law enforcers speeding and choppering towards the national disaster unfolding at the Mount Karver canteen.

Pam Bird is clearly embarrassed by her cohort's behaviour; you can sense her empathy as she takes down everyone's details. Finally she gets to you.

Just as you are saying *Michael O'Dell*, Constable Johnstone reappears. He glances over Pam's shoulder. 'How's Rosie?' he asks.

A lurch of dread, then a rush of hatred.

You'd like to grab Lance by the throat and choke the life out of him. There are a million things you'd like to say about bullying and thuggery and his appalling treatment of your daughter.

But your son is standing behind you. And other people's sons and daughters too. And you know how cruel and disproportionate this guy can be. He has spent the last fifteen minutes refreshing you on the subject of his stupidity. This makes you afraid.

'Fine thanks,' you say.

'Settling down a bit, is she?'

Bastard. 'She's doing well thanks.'

Pam Bird is obviously wondering who the hell Rosie is but neither of you offers an explanation. You're desperately trying to think of a way to shut this conversation down when the squad car radio burbles at them.

While Constable Johnstone answers the call, one of the kids asks Constable Bird if it's okay to continue filming and she says she supposes it is. Pam suggests you put up signs saying you are filming. You direct her attention to the two large signs that Declan has already taped either side of the canteen entrance saying: QUIET PLEASE, FILMING INSIDE.

Declan asks if there's any chance you could have the gun back so they can finish shooting the rest of the scene. Constable Bird looks at you, imploring you with her eyes to be mindful of the madman in the squad car behind her. She says, quietly, that they are confiscating the gun for the time being. Declan is about to appeal, but you turn to him and say, 'Declan,' with enough authority to silence him.

Constable Johnstone returns and tells you he and Constable Bird have to go now, like that's something you'd be sad about. He tells you he'll be taking up the matter with school security. He says that he may need to ask more questions in a couple of days.

And then finally, blessedly, he leaves.

You fashion a new gun from black tape, a block of wood and a cigarette lighter. It looks fine in the wide shots. Filming continues without incident.

17

Three days after the Mount Karver debacle, Constable Johnstone calls to inform you that the toy gun is officially classified as an illegal firearm. You express polite consternation and tell him that it is your understanding that the gun fires only potato pellets. Constable Johnstone says, yes, this is true but because the gun is an exact replica of a Glock pistol, it's illegal. He asks you where you got it. You tell him that you have no idea; you assume someone borrowed it for use during filming. He asks you to be more specific. You tell him that you are unable to be more specific and that you will need to make further inquiries. He instructs you not to make further inquiries; that's his job.

Then he asks you to come down to the station to discuss the matter at your earliest convenience. Your stomach flips and you tell him you'll get back to him.

As soon as Wendy walks through the door, you debrief. Wendy says no one from this family is going anywhere near that nutter and you realise with amazement that you were actually considering complying with his request.

What is wrong with you?

Wendy calls Shelley Mainwaring who laughs and can't believe your luck in coming up against the same crazy cop twice. She tells Wendy that she'll give him a call and have a chat. There's a lawyer—cop dialect that ordinary mortals don't speak and she feels confident she can sort out this minor incident in no time. She signs off, promising to phone Constable Johnstone immediately. She'll call back in five minutes.

You wait by the phone with Wendy. Five minutes pass. Ten minutes, fifteen. Half an hour. *Maybe Shelley has forgotten to call back.* Wendy calls Shelley; Shelley is engaged. The phone finally rings an hour later. Wendy races to answer it and by the time you reach the study she's talking to Shelley.

Shelley is in a state of shock. She's met some strange and bent cops in her time but the only expression she can find for Lance Johnstone is 'whack-job'.

'He's a whack-job. A total whack-job,' she declares.

Not only is he a whack-job, he's furious that you have not come down to the station as he requested, so he is on his way to your house to *arrest you for supply and possession of an illegal firearm!*

You babble an astonished protest via Wendy until she surrenders the phone and you talk directly to Shelley. Shelley tells you to calm down, which has the opposite effect. She tells you to leave the house immediately. Take the kids with you or farm them out to friends.

'For how long?' you ask.

If you had any doubts that you were not in a Kafka novel, Shelley's answer confirms it. 'Three hours,' she says.

Constable Lance Johnstone's shift ends at 10pm. After that he's on ten days' leave. So all you have to do is stay out until Lance's shift ends. No one else will come to arrest you because this is Constable Johnstone's case. Shelley feels confident that during the constable's holiday she will be able to make representations to stop you being arrested. She makes an appointment to see you at 10am in her office and reminds you to hurry: the crazy cop is on his way.

You and Wendy bundle the kids into the car and drop them at friends' houses. Then you drive across town to the newly renovated terrace house of your architect chum, Felipe, and his wife, Jools. They stare at you both, eyes widening, as you double-act the story thus far.

Jools says it would be funny if it weren't so serious. Both of them assure you that this will not, cannot, end badly. Felipe reminds you that we do not live in the kind of country where well-intentioned parents are bundled off to prison because their child uses a BB gun during the filming of a school drama project.

You know what they are saying makes perfect sense and, if it weren't happening to you, you'd be more inclined to be comforted by their certainty. But frankly you have no idea what kind of country you live in anymore. You seem to have slipped into an alternative universe, an Alice-less Wonderland of mad hunters and random outcomes.

A surge of panic dries your mouth. You get up and pour yourself a glass of water at the gleaming new stainless-steel double-bowled kitchen sink. You look into the frosty blackness of the freshly glazed kitchen window, fully expecting a monster to lunge at you. Instead the terrible secret flashes its ugly truth once again: *The good part of your life is over. The bad part has begun.*

At midnight you drive home and park outside the neighbours'. Wrapped up against an icy wind, Wendy checks the house while you stay in the car, feeling frightened and foolish, ready to make a getaway. Your brave wife establishes that no one is lurking in the bushes waiting to pounce and arrest you.

You go inside, shivering.

Egg leaps and wags a joyous greeting. You inquire whether he has anything to report. 'Woof,' he says, but does not elaborate.

Shelley Mainwaring surprises you by looking exactly as you pictured her. She's a short, slim woman with close-cropped brown hair and buoyant breasts that make you wonder whether they've been surgically enhanced. She's wearing a mushroom-coloured outfit with a pencil skirt that ends just below her knees. You have no idea whether this is fashionable or not but it suits her, in an I'm-smart-and-bossy-but-haven't-given-up-on-sexy kind of way.

You can see that Wendy likes and trusts this woman so you decide to trust your wife's impeccable taste and trust her too. Shelley explains that Constable Johnstone is no doubt trying to justify his overreaction on the day of the gun incident by making things appear more serious than they are. She says that your biggest mistake was nominating yourself as the responsible adult. Constable Johnstone has decided you are responsible for everything that happened, whether it happened with your knowledge or not.

Shelley says the best thing to do is supply the police with a signed statement so they can see you were just a concerned dad helping your son with a school project. She asks you to tell her what happened on the day of filming prior to the arrival of the police. She starts to guide you with a few simple questions. You try to answer but you're so rattled that you leap through the story to what you believe is the salient bit: you neither own nor supplied the firearm! Declan borrowed the gun from his old primary school mate, Dan. Dan's dad purchased the gun as a gift in Hong Kong. Dan's dad didn't declare it to Customs because he thought it was a toy. When Declan came home with the gun the night before the shoot, you gave it little more than a cursory glance because it was a toy.

As you offer this information, you find yourself stammering for the first time in your life. Your tongue catches on words like t-t-toy. You talk so fast that phrases crash into one another in little collisions: 'Dansdad purshasedthegun asag-g-gift.'

Wendy gives you a what's-going-on look. You take a deep breath and try to slow down. Your hands are shaking. You try to stop them but you can't. You tell yourself it's only the slightest tremor; no one will notice. But you see that Shelley has noticed.

And then she does the worst thing she could possibly do: she's kind to you. She asks gently if you'd like to take a short break. You feel tears spring to your eyes and once again you curse your emotional incontinence. You ask for the toilets and make your escape.

In the toilets, you fight those unmanly tears with great gasps of angry air. Eventually you can breathe normally and are able to return.

During your absence, Wendy has told Shelley about your accident. Shelley says she can see that you are stressed and that this is perfectly understandable but wonders whether your reaction has been exacerbated by the recent trauma of your car accident. She asks if you've heard of post-traumatic stress disorder.

You can see where this is going so you tell her, yeah, you've read plenty about post-traumatic stress disorder in relation to the troops returning from Afghanistan and you'd be embarrassed to compare your lot with theirs. The modulated vehemence in your reply dissuades Shelley from pursuing the matter any further.

You wait while Shelley drafts a version of your statement. In no time at all you are reading about the incident as you related it to her. You notice how it has been crafted not to implicate any other individual—not Declan, not Dan, not Dan's dad—while shouting via subtext, 'It's not Michael O'Dell's fault! It's got nothing to do with Michael O'Dell!'

*

A few hours later Shelley calls you at home to let you know that she has personally delivered the statement to the police station. The cops have indicated that it may not be sufficient and you may be required for further questioning. You ask Shelley how this will play out. She doesn't know. But she signs off with the following advice: in the unlikely (she stresses *unlikely* as if it's going to comfort you) event that the police try to arrest you again, surrender peacefully but do not make any statement until she is in the room with you.

You thank her politely while your other, inner voice screams, *Arrest? Are you fucking kidding me?*

Wendy slumps at the kitchen table doing the accounts, tapping away at a spreadsheet on her laptop, occasionally pausing to consult a large pile of unpaid bills. Hearing you enter the room, she picks up a bill and hands it to you. You read it. It's from Mainwaring, Pollard and Van Der Smagt. For Shelley's legal services. For $2800.

'What? I thought we were getting mates' rates!'

'These are mates' rates. I think.'

'We can't afford that!'

'We have to pay it.'

'How are we going to pay the mortgage then?'

'That's what I'm trying to figure out.'

You sit down next to your wife. You stare at each other, waiting for a solution to materialise in the anxious air between you. You know you should be grateful that you do not live in a war zone and that your children have all their fingers and toes but all you can think is *Why me? Why this extra little kick in the head? Like I haven't had enough kicks in the head lately.*

'When's the mortgage due?'

'Wednesday.' 'Shit.'

'I'm going to call Mum. Ask her for a loan. Just to get us through this next payment.'

'Thanks. That's good. But it's not a solution.'

'No.'

You are impotent and inadequate, your inner voice tells you. *The least you could do is get a job stocking supermarket shelves.*

'We need to think about selling the house,' Wendy says.

You know what it costs her to say this so matter-of-factly and you feel a part of your soul collapsing. All you can do is nod. 'We can't do anything now,' she adds. 'Let's try and hang on till Declan finishes his exams. We'll get some estate agents through to have a look after the exams. And let's not tell the kids. God, we mustn't let the kids find out.'

Down the back of your garden the lawn leads to a large sandstone platform about the size of a small room. A huge tree reaches over it, casting fractured shadows over its brown carpet of fallen leaves. Resting against the trunk is a rotting timber bench, orphaned from an outdoor setting you bought when there was money spare to spend on such things.

You lower yourself onto the bench. It groans under your weight, threatening, as usual, to collapse. Although you suppose that one day it will, you are inured to its complaints and take no notice. You stare across the decaying paling fence at the densely vegetated valley beyond. If all the shrubs and palms were cleared away, you would see hundreds of houses on quarter-acre blocks stretching away before you, but even in the depths of winter the garden is so abundant that you cannot see your neighbour's roof. It's dark and damp and quiet here.

Someone takes your hand. You assume that it's Wendy but turn to discover Rosie sitting next to you. She is observing you. She sees that you are broken. You wonder if this is *that moment*, the moment when the child realises that the parent is human, flawed, fallible, scrambling like everyone else to make sense of the unmakesensible.

You are no longer big, strong, dependable Daddy. Daddy who puts a roof over our heads and brings home money for food and clothes. Daddy who fixes things and makes things better. Daddy who knows best.

Oh, who are you kidding? You never were.

Rosie lifts your hand to her lips and kisses it. It's an impossibly tender gesture, one of forgiveness, you hope, for all that you have failed to do. Both of you know better than to try and form words, so you sit in silence. You sit in silence until the sky washes orange and mauve and tiny insects hatch from the rotting leaves, biting your ankles.

Rosie slaps her arm. 'Let's go in,' she says, and you follow her up the yard.

18

It's Sunday night, 9.40pm. Five blocks north of your house, a group of teenagers straggle home from the shops where they've managed to procure an assortment of beer and alco-pop beverages. Most likely they've spent the evening in the tiny triangle of park near the train station, hiding behind the azalea bushes where they can drink without being disturbed.

Jason Lind, the Boomerang dad who warned you about the Pessites, is having a secret smoke in his front garden when a few of the tipsy teens pass his gate, arguing. A tall boy in a blue beanie turns on another in a red windcheater and punches him on the arm. Red Windcheater goes to retaliate but trips and falls in the gutter. Blue Beanie laughs and runs across the road where he collects a slap from Pretty Blonde teetering in high heels. There's yelling and shouting and more running across the road.

It's a busy road, Jason's road, a minor arterial that stretches from the highway south to a major arterial. It's only two lanes but even at this time on Sunday night there's a trickle of traffic. Jason worries. With three girls of his own (all watching telly inside, thank God), he knows that the combination of dark night, drunk teens and fast cars can lead somewhere bad. Jason wonders whether he shouldn't give the cops a friendly call, make sure these kids get home safe and sound. Jason hears a bottle break. That settles it.

Jason goes inside, washes his face and gargles minty mouthwash so Polly and the kids won't smell the smoke. He calls the local police station. While he's on the phone, Polly smells smoke on Jason's shirtsleeve and institutes a search for his hidden cigarettes. She'll never find them—they're in a zip-lock bag in the spare tyre well of their station wagon— but that won't stop her from spending the rest of the evening trying and tsking.

Seven blocks south of your house, Rosie and Juan are hurrying home. It's 9.51pm, a school day tomorrow, and their curfew is 10pm. They've been watching a DVD at Rosie's friend's house. Mimi and Rosie were best buddies in primary school and, although they attend different high schools, the friendship has prospered. Mimi's parents, Andrea and Phillip von Trotsenberger, are stalwarts of the local community and it comforts you to think Rosie is in their sphere of influence. You know either Phillip or Andrea will have sent Rosie on her way at 9.40pm precisely, allowing for the seventeen minutes it takes to walk from their house to yours.

Simultaneously, Rosie and Juan notice a police wagon driving towards them. Rosie feels a rush of dread and resentment.

'Shit,' says Juan quietly. He's done nothing wrong but his dark skin, multiple piercings and buzz haircut are a walking proclamation of guilt. Rosie has reported often and with indignation how Juan is regarded with suspicion by anyone in charge of anything—shopkeepers, stationmasters, cinema attendants, policemen. She is appalled by the racism she constantly witnesses in his presence. Juan, sadly, is used to it. Which is not the same thing as being comfortable with it.

The police wagon passes and Juan exhales a puff of warm white air that punctuates the cold night. Rosie releases the grip she has on his forearm, only then realising that she has grabbed him in the first place.

Suddenly there's a burst of red from the wagon's brake lights. It stops and begins to reverse. Somewhere in the limbic core of Juan's brain, his flight or fight response kicks in. Juan chooses flight and runs. The police wagon skids to a halt and two officers fly out. One grabs Rosie by the arm while the other chases Juan down a driveway. By the time the cop reaches the back fence, Juan is long gone; he's three gardens away leaping fences, pumping with enough adrenaline to keeping him running for another thirty-five minutes; he'll eventually stop four suburbs away.

On the footpath, Rosie demands to be released. The cop lets her go. This guy is young and handsome in a predictable movie-star kind of way and his badge identifies him as Sergeant Matt Vass. Matt wants to know why Juan took flight.

Rosie offers the furious and simple explanation, 'Because you freaked him out!' She demands to know what they've done wrong.

Matt Vass is beginning to suspect that Rosie has done nothing wrong. He can't smell alcohol on her breath and she's behaving in a coherent if aggressive manner. He asks her a few questions to establish that she's not part of the drunken teen group who've been running into the traffic and breaking bottles further up the street. Clearly she's not.

Matt's partner returns huffing and puffing and Matt tells Rosie to wait there while they have a quick chat. Rosie says she has a ten o'clock curfew, she's not waiting, she's going home. Matt tells her to wait there and goes to talk to his partner. Rosie starts to walk away. Matt grabs her arm. Rosie tries to wrest it away. Matt's partner grabs Rosie's other arm. Rosie struggles. Matt tells her to calm down. Rosie screams. A porch light comes on and a neighbour rushes out to see what's going on.

At 10.14pm on Sunday night, you're watching TV in the living room, sitting in the old painted cane chairs that look as if they belong in someone else's beach house. You can't remember when they appeared and you suppose they are Wendy's attempt at bohemian chic, but privately you think they look like junkshop refuse. Nonetheless, they're a lot more comfortable than sitting on the floor so you keep your interior design opinions to your interior.

Also, you don't care.

And you don't care that you don't care. You have absolutely no interest in what you think. For the last few days you've been bobbing around once more in your swamp of self-loathing. You find yourself so useless and pointless that it would take your breath away if you weren't already so bored by yourself that you couldn't be bothered making the effort of a disbelieving gasp.

The doorbell rings. You assume it's Rosie and Juan returning a little past curfew *but who gives a flying fuck. If Wendy does, she can deal with it.* 'It's open,' you call out. The doorbell rings again. You listen to see if Wendy is coming to answer it. She isn't. Irritated, you lift yourself out of the cane chair and open the front door.

A policeman is standing there.

It's after 10pm on Sunday night and a policeman is standing at your front door. Both Declan and Rosie are out. You are immediately certain that one of them is dead. Your soul shatters. You're a dead man waiting for a policeman to tell you what you already know.

Sergeant Matt Vass tries to explain what is happening but something about the big blond bloke he's talking to tells him it's not really registering.

The cop seems to be telling you that he has Rosie in the back of the police wagon. He says she is refusing to get out; she keeps screaming that her poor family have been through enough. She is demanding to be taken to prison.

This makes no sense, which, of course, makes perfect sense because nothing in your life makes sense anymore. You accompany the cop down to his wagon where his partner opens the rear doors to reveal Rosie clinging to the metal grid, wild-eyed.

And that's the last thing you remember, for a while anyway.

Twelve hours later, after you have been medicated and are sitting in the psychiatrist's office, Wendy will relate a version of your lost minutes as reported to her by Sergeant Vass.

According to the sergeant, you climb into the back of the wagon and calmly ask Rosie to get out. Rosie, who appears to be transfixed by demons from another dimension, does not respond. You ask again. Again she does not respond.

You do not ask a third time. Instead, you try to pry sobbing Rosie's lovely fingers from the slim bars of the metal grid that encases the rear of the wagon.

She won't let go.

So you howl like a wounded animal and slam your hands on the metal cage of the wagon with such ferocity that your palms bleed. Startled by this inexplicable turn of events, Matt Vass grabs your hands and drags you out of the wagon. You do not resist but continue to howl.

Wendy hears the howling and races outside to see what on earth is going on.

The next thing you remember, you are back inside and two young cops are using all their strength to push you down into the cane chair where you sit, broken.

Matt Vass takes Wendy outside to the cold concrete

veranda and asks, with a lowered voice, if there are any domestic violence issues he should be aware of. Wendy sees where he is heading and feels a surge of panic. As lucidly as possible, she tries to explain the series of unfortunate events that have led to this moment. She tries to strip the desperation out of her voice but she can't.

'Are you okay?' Matt Vass asks.

'Yes.'

'Are you sure?'

'Yes.'

'Are you safe?'

'Yes.'

'Are you sure you're safe?'

On it goes, with Wendy reassuring him that she and Rosie are not captive in the lair of a domestic monster.

'I really should report this incident,' says Matt.

'Please don't. It's not how it looks. Please don't.'

A combination of experience and instinct tells Matt Vass that Wendy is not bound to silence by terror nor is she trying to conceal some dark truth from him. He agrees to let the matter rest but not before he gives her a card with his contact details and extracts a promise that she will call him should the need arise.

He asks one final time, 'And you're sure you're okay?' Then he heads down the sandstone steps that lead to the gravel driveway where his partner waits patiently by the police wagon.

Utterly drained, Wendy closes the front door and looks into the living room to find you gently rocking Rosie in your arms.

In other circumstances this might strike her as a charming if unorthodox portrait of a father with an oversized daughter in his lap. But the rocking is eerily mechanical and Rosie's eyes are squeezed shut. 'MakeitstopDaddymakeitstop, MakeitstopDaddymakeitstop, MakeitstopDaddymakeitstop,' she says. 'MakeitstopDaddymakeitstop, Makeitstop Daddymakeitstop, MakeitstopDaddymakeitstop…'

Wendy moves quickly to the kitchen, opens a kitchen cupboard and cries quietly into the door. She wonders whether to break them up, her crazy husband and her mad daughter, but decides to let them be.

Eventually Rosie falls asleep and Wendy lifts her from your arms. She does not notice the weight of her almost-grown daughter as she carries her to bed. The calamity battering at her domestic ramparts is all consuming. Details that would once have preoccupied her—'Argh! You're too heavy for me to carry; you're a big girl now'—don't even register.

Wendy returns to the living room to find you still rocking back and forth to the same strange mechanical rhythm. She tells you that it's frightening her, but you don't even hear her.

Only when your wife kneels in front of you and puts her hands on your knees do you see her. You look down at her face that is blurred with tears and snot.

'Please,' she begs softly, 'Stop. You're scaring me.'

But you don't stop. You say, 'This isn't about you.'

You don't mean this in a nasty way but it comes out like that and, horribly, the exchange disintegrates into a brief but vicious fight. As is often the way with this genre of domestic drama, the tragedy climaxes in an absurdly comedic moment as you hiss at Wendy in a silly Gollum voice, 'Leave me alone. Leave me alone. Leave me alone…'

You sit in silence for a while with Wendy crumpled at your feet. She says matter-of-factly that she can't leave you alone because she's worried that you will kill yourself. And as usual she's kind of right. You don't want to kill yourself but oblivion seems a seductive option. *If you could just slip away into nothingness…*

… if you could just slip away.

'Annie,' you announce with sudden certainty. 'Get Annie.'

'Annie?' says Wendy, surprised.

Annie has been Wendy's best friend since they met at school in Year 7. The bond deepened between them when they turned thirteen and both fell in love with the same beret-wearing boy, who attended a private Steiner school just down the road from their school.

Both girls took to staying on the morning bus two stops past their school with the sole objective of breathing the same air as Beret Boy. When Beret Boy disembarked, the girls would also disembark, then cross the road and catch another bus back to school. They never actually spoke to him but remained ever-hopeful that he might notice them, which, apparently, he never did.

With an iron-willed persistence that would come as no surprise to anyone who encountered their older selves, young Annie and Wendy convinced their respective parents that a Steiner education was critical to their intellectual development. They both changed schools and ended up a class below

Beret Boy, who continued to act as if he didn't notice they existed because, of course, he didn't.

When they tell you this story years later at university you ask what happened to Beret Boy.

They both stop and think for a moment and shrug.

'But don't you want to know?' you press them.

'Nup,' says Annie.

'Not really,' says Wendy.

'So you have no interest in the fate of someone who shaped your educational destiny and changed the course of your lives forever?' you ask.

Both consider the froth on their cappuccinos. They look up at you and simultaneously answer, 'Nope.'

You ask for Annie to come and sit with you because, in no particular order:

(a) Your wife is worn out. You have worn her out.

(b) Annie lives around the corner and although she's a single mum her three boys are old enough to be left, particularly if she's just around the corner at your place.

(c) Annie is kind and dependable. There is not a crazy, neurotic, judgmental bone in her body. And she's solid. Tonight, if you are not going to slip into the abyss, you need to anchor yourself to someone solid.

Tonight, if you are not going to slip into the abyss, you need to anchor yourself to someone solid.

That's your new mantra as you rock back and forth on the

couch until at some point you realise that Annie is sitting next to you, holding your hand, while Egg is at your feet.

You sit this way all night, in and out of states of conscious and unconscious despair so dark and terrible that you intermittently startle awake, whimpering. Each time you wake Annie is there. She squeezes your hand, holding you in life. Egg is there too.

In the grim abyss, you hear a dim but certain pulse:

I am life, it beats.

You are life, it beats.

We are the same thing. I will not let you go. You will not be extinguished.

Early next morning, Wendy takes Rosie to the clinic at St Jude's where the pretty young psychologist always says she's doing fine. Wendy insists on being in the session to make sure Rosie relates every detail of the previous night's episode. Rosie tells all, a strangely dispassionate narrator. The psychologist takes it in and asks Rosie how she feels about it.

'Fine,' she answers.

Wendy turns to Rosie, astonished.

Rosie snaps, 'What? Don't you want me to be fine?'

Wendy's eyes fill with tears. Rosie's bottom lip quivers. She starts to cry. There's nothing restrained or delicate about her ugly, eyes-scrunched, heart-rending howl. Wendy puts her arms around her daughter and pulls her close. Rosie collapses into her mother's embrace and they sob together.

By 11am Rosie is home in bed, telling an unconvinced Annie

that she is feeling a lot better. Meanwhile, you are sitting on a psychiatrist's couch, floating on a medicated cloud of numb. Wendy is back on duty, relating your police-wagon escapades to Doctor Maurice O'Connell.

Despite her harrowing morning, your wife has managed to pull some strings and locate a shrink who has agreed to see you immediately. He has injected you with something to reduce your anxiety, diagnosed you with post-traumatic stress disorder, prescribed antidepressants and assured you that in the next couple of weeks the clouds will start to lift, all before you can say *ticketyboo*.

Your first session is over and Doctor Maurice ushers you out into the waiting room where Wendy sits on a minimal-ist Italian leather couch flicking through a magazine. It is only then that you realise she must have left you alone with Doctor O'Connell. Before she looks up you scan the room, with its high ceilings, recessed lighting, elaborate ceiling rose, exclusive designer furniture and palette of colours that some marketing team has spent days naming Driftwood, Dry Bone and Chocolate Drizzle. Everything tells you that you are probably inside an expensively restored nineteenth-century terrace house, somewhere in the inner city.

When you go outside the streetscape confirms your diagnosis. How the hell did you drive all the way into the city centre without noticing where you were going? Luckily the haze of drugs does not encourage you to probe any further. It does not occur to you to enquire how you can afford to pay a shrink who can afford such fancy real estate because the answer would make you crazier than you already are.

19

You are in the study trying to write about the proliferation of
visual effects companies in the early 2000s, when you smell
your socks burning. You switch off the bar heater at your feet
and wiggle your hot toes, feeling a pang of guilt about the
unnecessary expense, especially since the weather is warming.
Wendy is having even more trouble juggling bills now that
you are paying for a shrink, and you're equal parts ashamed
and grateful that she is keeping the details of your financial
floundering to herself.

You hear the front door open and Wendy greet Declan.
Your wife is upbeat and warm but a sudden change in
her tone tells you something is up. You hear her coolly
inquiring where your son has been, whom he has been
with, and whether he intends to do any homework. You

strain to hear Declan's response but all that comes is the usual mumble.

You hear Declan head down the hall to his room and then Wendy appears at the study door.

'He's stoned.'

'You sure?'

'Pupils the size of saucers and he stinks of it.'

'Shit.'

'I can't believe he's started again.'

'Maybe it's a one-off. Things have been pretty stressy around here.'

'That would be the understatement of the century.'

You see a plan of action form on Wendy's face and she disappears down the hall, where she passes Declan. She tries to make eye contact with him but he suspects his eyes have already betrayed him and is careful not to look at her again.

'Where are you going?' she interrogates.

'Having a shower.' His articulation is unusually precise.

Declan disappears into the bathroom and Wendy heads into his bedroom where she executes a full search-and-recovery operation. It doesn't take her long to discover another home-made bong hidden under the bed.

Every now and then the ancient tree-fern that towers over your swimming pool is overcome by the urge to reproduce. It showers the world with tiny brown spores that clog the pool filter and layer the windowsills with a veil of dirty gold dust.

Today the French doors are open in an attempt to capture some late winter sun, and the spores venture inside. They settle on the honey-coloured timber of the kitchen table. With his hair still dripping from the shower, Declan uses a single finger to sweep the fine film of spores into little brown piles along the table-top. Wendy asks him to look at her. He looks up.

Wendy tells him that she wouldn't mind so much if the dope just made him giggly and gave him the munchies. But we all know (she says, nodding to include you) that is not the case. 'The dope makes you depressed, Declan. Dangerously depressed.'

You have chosen not to sit with Wendy and Declan but to hover by the kitchen sink where you nod as Wendy speaks. You are like one of those nodding toy dogs in the rear windows of cars. Your articulated head bobs back and forth as you witness the proceedings through the smog of your medication.

Declan listens to his mother, compliant and defeated. He's still a little stoned and knows better than to argue with her when he's not at full capacity. He reminds you for all the world of a floppy doll; you could arrange his limbs in any configuration you liked and they would remain that way until you decided to rearrange them.

Wendy is unusually frank with Declan. She tells him that the family is disintegrating and that she cannot cope with him smoking pot. He promises to stop.

'Promise me.'

'I promise.'

They are the only words he utters and when he says them, the smog clears. You see that the kid is completely overwhelmed. He doesn't need anyone to tell him his family is disintegrating; he knows. All the certainties of childhood have abandoned him—and at the worst possible time. Just as he is facing his final exams and preparing for the next great leap forward—to university and beyond—a chasm has opened up in front of him. And, because of your inability to cope with the unfortunate events that have befallen you, you have flooded the chasm with chaos.

You're looking at Wendy as she's holding your newborn son in her arms. Her face is sweaty and deathly pale but she emanates an intoxicating combination of exhaustion and jubilation.

It's been a long, hard labour: twenty hours of intense contractions because the baby is facing the wrong way and pressing against her spine; a show of muddy mucus that indicates the baby is in distress, shitting himself inside the womb; a slowing foetal heart rate; preparations for an emergency Caesarean abandoned when the foetal heart rate suddenly ceases; a child ripped from his mother with what looks like a giant pair of barbecue tongs; a silent, bluish baby; his mother calling out, 'Why isn't he crying? Why isn't he crying?' as the doctors huddle over him in a corner; and eventually, blessedly, the furious scream of a pinking newborn.

That glorious howling sweeps the trauma away. You are filled with the inestimable joy of watching your son. Wendy looks up at you with a wicked grin. 'So this perfect little person has arrived and now we get to fuck him up.'

A release valve opens, laughter bubbles from both of you and washes over your tiny boy. A quip delivered flippantly, it nonetheless feels profoundly true.

You see Rosie dancing up the gravel drive, executing pirouettes, waving a white envelope above her head. Juan laughs and claps and tries to snatch the envelope but she whips it away from him, leaping and twirling. Egg joins in the fun, barking and running in circles. From your position at the bedroom window, you find that the muscles of your face have arranged themselves into a smile, which must mean, of course, that you are happy.

The envelope contains a letter that, for once, *praise the Lord*, brings some good news: Rosie has been shortlisted for next year's intake into Mount Karver. Rosie and her parents have been invited to an interview with the headmaster. If she gets in—which she probably will because Declan is already there—she will leave Boomerang and make a fresh start for her final three years of schooling.

Declan enters and Rosie babbles the news at him and you brace yourself for his response. But he just grins at her and they high-five. Rosie throws her arms around him and he kisses the top of her head and tells her that she is going to love it. You silently bless your son and give thanks for his open-heartedness. Wendy looks over at you and you see that her eyes are bright with tears.

Spring dawdles erratically into September: it's warm, then cold, freezing for a morning, then hot for a week. In the garden, some plants burst into activity, others sleep late and wake confused. The peach tree outside your bedroom window begins to fruit while the peach at the letterbox is just starting to blossom. Your miniature American azaleas flower but their larger Japanese cousins remain shyly in bud. There's not going to be a ta-da moment this year; it's the botanical equivalent of every man for himself.

As Declan's final exams draw closer, he seems to be studying less and less. Wendy initiates a program where he brings his books to the kitchen table and works under her watchful eye. Sometimes she joins him at the table, doing her own work.

Sometimes she prompts him as she prepares dinner. 'Have you finished your maths revision?' 'What page are you on?' 'You've been on that page for a while, haven't you?'

As the questions proceed, an ambience of general annoyance sets in. Declan is annoyed by the questions. Wendy is annoyed by having to ask them. But there is no question that Wendy must indeed *ask* the questions. Declan is capable of staring at a page for fifteen minutes without reading a word. They both know this but it doesn't stop the situation from becoming unbearable.

Within a couple of weeks Declan is irritated by the mere sight of his mother and takes to avoiding her. Whenever she forces an interaction he answers in a bored monotone, which clearly hurts her feelings. You snap at him not to speak to his mother like that and Wendy snaps at you because you are not being helpful.

*

Your niece, Mel, is ten years older than Declan and he adores her. You all adore her because she enlivens your house with her funny stories and infectious laughter. Mel is a qualified teacher but is currently completing a PhD in psychology with the intention of becoming a school counsellor. She's looking for part-time work until she graduates at the end of the year and so it seems the perfect solution to offer Mel a job as Declan's tutor.

She comes each day as he arrives home from school. Together they complete the ritual of afternoon tea and then commence a couple of hours' study before dinner. You hear them bantering as Mel asks pretty much the same questions that Wendy asked only days earlier. Only now there are peals of laughter and furtive giggles and long periods of silence while actual work is done.

'Read that paragraph.'

'I've read it.'

'Okay. Turn the page and read the next one. And don't you roll your eyes at me.'

Declan flicks Mel's pen across the table. It clatters onto the floor. Mel punches him on the shoulder and tells him to pick it up. He holds her gaze, smirking, and then scrambles on the floor for longer than is necessary to retrieve the pen. He resurfaces and attempts to balance the pen on his nose. Mel removes the pen and points to the page. Declan reads. And so the miracle unfolds—Declan studies without resenting you for making him do it.

Mel has an inkling of your financial position and tries to refuse payment. She usually stays for dinner and attempts to mount a case that this is adequate compensation. You argy-bargy back and forth and eventually settle on an hourly rate that is far below what she is worth and far above what you can afford. Later, when you discuss this with Wendy, she remains strangely silent. When you press her she says, 'I don't know how we're going to pay for it.'

You don't know how you're going to pay for it either, until Ingrid calls and says Mel has told her about coaching Declan. She says that she thinks it's a great idea but she knows things can't be easy financially. 'So why don't you borrow a few grand from your cashed-up big sister,' she asks, 'just to tide you over?'

You don't even make a pretence of refusing. Knowing you're feeling uncomfortable about it, though, Ingrid adds, 'I know you'd do the same for me, kiddo.' If she were standing in front of you, you would kiss her feet.

When you tell your architect friend Felipe about your niece's daily sessions he accuses you of outsourcing your parenting responsibilities.

'It's your job to make sure your kid sits down and does his work,' says Felipe, 'not your niece's.'

You suppose he's right but you don't care because it's working. And anyway there's something about Mel being your niece, about keeping it in the family, that makes it seem okay.

Later, in the shower, it occurs to you that in many societies, extended families play this role in the raising of children. Aunts, uncles, cousins and grandparents all muck in to share the load with parents. You make a mental note to tell Felipe that he is pigeonholing you as the patriarch of a nuclear family when really you are engaged in a much broader family structure. You're imagining the defeated look on Felipe's face as you tell him this when you realise that Felipe won't actually give a flying fig. Felipe will, in fact, have completely forgotten the conversation. Felipe pretended to be excited by your hospital ceilings epiphany but had no clue what you were talking about when you raised it during the crazy cop crisis.

What a sad little man you have become, financed by your wife and big sister, gloating over non-existent victories in the bathroom mirror.

20

Despite the veil of medication—or possibly because of it—you are able to write again. You don't care whether it's good or bad; you're glad to be writing again.

Actually that's not true. You care deeply whether it's good or bad but you know that it's important to let the words pour out. The words have come just when you thought they might never come again. If you continually ask yourself the dreaded question, *But is this good enough?* you will stem the flow. So you write. You just write.

The local paper, *Village Voice*, takes two of your reviews for recent movies and asks you to do a regular column on the art-house-ish movies run by the independent cinema a few suburbs from your home. The money isn't great but it helps with some of the bills. Wendy is relieved and, not that Ingrid asks, but it feels good to tell your sister that you are generating income. It also gives you the confidence boost you need to return to 'serious' writing—your book.

Or so you think.

You decide to begin work on your chapter about Australian movie stars. You have interviewed most of them before and have all the relevant contact details for their publicists and managers, so you start to write emails requesting interviews. As part of the request, you try to paint a picture of what your book is about in broad brushstrokes.

And this is where you come undone.

Every time you attempt to do this, you sound like a self-important wanker. Again and again you try to strike an engaging tone but it all ends in a horrible road accident of not-quite-the-right adjectives colliding in overly elaborate sentences.

You ask yourself whether this is a symptom of a larger disease; maybe you can't construct a strong paragraph about your book because you don't really know what your book is about. Or maybe you know what your book is about but you don't have clear enough vision to write it. Or maybe you have no talent and should just go back to bed.

Ah, yes, that's it.

You have no talent. You *did* once but it's gone. It was run over by a car and died.

You take your worn copy of *Zorba the Greek* from the shelf. It's a touchstone book for you; every couple of years you re-read it for inspiration. You love the vivid language but most of all you love the character of Zorba. With his joyful, irrepressible lust for life, he is, in your opinion, one of the great characters of literature. And cinema; you loved the movie too.

Once Felipe asked to borrow *Zorba* and you handed it over reluctantly. Felipe didn't read it but his wife Jools did. She told Felipe it was a load of misogynistic twaddle. You can see where she's coming from but you think she missed the point. You prefer to think of it as a celebration of spiritedness. And a window into a pre-feminist world. As far as you're concerned, Zorba is *the man*.

You open to one of your favorite passages, hoping to vanish into the glorious prose, but it doesn't do the trick. You decide to clean your keyboard instead.

Days later you try to describe your writing crisis to your psychiatrist, Doctor Maurice, but even as you hear yourself crapping on about it, you are disgusted by its lack of importance in the grand scheme of things. You confess how embarrassed you are to be making such a fuss when far worse things are happening to people every day—to the war-torn, the sick, the poor (to mention a few billion). And most of them just get on with it. *Why can't you?*

Doctor Maurice asks you to stop comparing yourself to everybody else—you can do that eventually but right now it is important for your recovery that you focus on yourself. You need to 'observe' what is happening to you and accept it. You don't need to 'attach' to the bad things that have happened; they don't have to 'define' you. But you need to 'walk around' the bad events in your life and say, 'This happened to me.'

Acknowledgement, he tells you, is the best way to move

forward. Currently you are so busy shouting 'Why aren't I better? I should be better!' that you are impeding your own recovery.

This makes sense, you suppose, so you decide to give it a whirl.

Rosie comes home, white and weepy. It takes you ages to coax any information out of her but it turns out that Eva Pessites has also applied to go to Mount Karver. Just when Rosie is about to make a fresh start at a new school, the very reason she needs to make a fresh start will be coming with her. Eva will poison this new well too.

'Well, if she goes to Mount Karver maybe you could stay at Boomerang.'

As soon as you say it, you know it's a dumb idea. Rosie groans and heads off to her room. You follow her down the hall with a second offering. 'Maybe she won't be accepted.'

Rosie looks at you in disbelief. 'Dad. It's Eva. She gets accepted into everything.'

21

Elsie Schmetterling (the German word for 'butterfly', she explains to practically everyone she meets) is the personal assistant to Mount Karver's headmaster, Doctor Ignatius Quinn. One very hot summer day three years ago, Elsie and Wendy engineered the canteen rosters together (Wendy as representative of the mothers committee) and they have been chummy ever since. She hugs Wendy warmly and appears to be thrilled to meet you and Rosie.

Elsie ushers you into a vast office where Doctor Quinn waits to greet you, standing at attention. Unlike Christina Bowden's room at Boomerang, this place is designed to impress. Where her office is cramped and practical, his is gleaming and cavernous; unless you are a sultan or an emperor or a curator of antiquities you are not important enough to be here.

Doctor Quinn settles you into a cluster of wingback chairs overlooking the immaculately manicured front lawn, where a flagpole sprouts from a bed of riotous pansies. An Australian flag flutters majestically in just the right amount of wind. The three of you watch in silence while the headmaster checks some papers on the mahogany acreage of his desk. Scanning the collection of period Australian art on the oak-panelled walls, you calculate that if you sold just half of them you could live like a king for the rest of your life.

Rosie takes a breath to calm her nerves. You wink reassuringly at her. Wendy clears her throat and the headmaster sinks into the wingback chair next to you. He moves quickly from the sound of the mower on the front lawn, to the smell of freshly cut grass, to the gun incident outside the canteen. You try to make light of it without sounding flippant but he unnerves you by revealing that the police are 'still making inquiries'.

'About what?' asks Wendy. 'Are they questioning students?'

They're not questioning students but they are talking to teachers, trying to determine the various procedures and permissions that allowed Declan to stage a fake robbery in the canteen. Apparently they are 'put out' because they weren't given the 'appropriate warning'.

'Appropriate warning?' you ask, feeling your hackles rise.

The headmaster is sympathetic, apologetic even, but wonders whether you may not have inflamed police interest by not allowing them to interview you directly. You didn't know he knew this. The police must have told him about your refusal to go into the station for questioning.

Wendy steps in to explain that the hysterical performance of the cop that day convinced you that you could not count on fair or rational treatment and that you therefore felt it wise to remove yourselves from the equation and place matters in the hands of legal counsel. She does not elaborate about your dealings with Constable Lance Johnstone and Rosie prior to the gun incident, or add that he is the last person on earth you would trust.

Doctor Quinn listens, nodding empathetically, before he expertly wraps up the conversation and moves on to the real reason for this meeting: Rosie's application for admission to Mount Karver.

As he turns his benign attention to your daughter, it strikes you that he is one of those people with a gift for making you feel like you are the only person in the room. He asks a couple of questions about Rosie's interest in drama and her prowess on the soccer field. (This is encouraging because you know that Mount Karver is keen to win the interschool girls soccer comp.)

Rosie answers in a forthright but modest way that neither seeks to impress nor downplays her achievements. You feel proud of your daughter, of how she is handling herself in these challenging circumstances. It's time for her to step up to the plate and that is exactly what she is doing.

Then, from out of nowhere, 'Do you get angry very much, Rose?' he asks.

You and Wendy exchange a look that says *Huh?*

'Do you ever get into fights?'

You and Wendy exchange a look that says *Uh-huh!*

Wendy stops the interview. She asks Rosie to go outside while you talk privately to Doctor Quinn. Rosie looks startled and even the headmaster looks a little rattled. As Rosie leaves the room, traversing three thick Persian carpets, you once again sit in silence until the huge oak door clicks shut behind her.

Wendy turns from the door to the headmaster and asks why he is pursuing this line of questioning. Doctor Quinn pauses and in that moment you know for certain that he knows about the fight with Eva Pessites and that he knows that you know that he knows.

Wendy asks whether anyone from Boomerang has spoken to him about Rosie.

This guy is no dummy. He's had years of managing tricky parents and you can't help but be a little awed by the way he ducks and weaves through Wendy's barrage of questions without giving any solid answers. You are left with three certainties:

(1) He will not admit that Christina Bowden or anyone from Boomerang has told him about the Eva altercation.

(2) He will not admit that Eva or anyone from her family has told him about the altercation.

(3) He knows all about the altercation.

Wendy is in an icy fury that she tries to conceal from Rosie as you drive home. Rosie sits in the back seat clinging to an optimistic view that, even though Doctor Quinn knows about the fight, she may still be admitted to Mount Karver. Although you sense that she hasn't got a hope in hell, you jolly her along because there is a remote possibility that she may be right.

Back at home, Rosie goes downstairs to debrief with Juan, and Wendy calls Christina Bowden, who assures her that no one from Boomerang has given details about the fight to anyone at Mount Karver. 'It would be prejudicial and unethical,' says Christina when Wendy presses her. 'We just wouldn't do it.' You both trust this woman, and conclude that either the police or the Pessites must have told the headmaster about the fight.

Constable Lance Johnstone is dumb, mean and unethical enough to snitch on Rosie but it's unlikely that he would have any idea about her application to Mount Karver and therefore would not know that information about the fight would be relevant to Doctor Quinn.

The most likely scenario is that the Pessites have described their version of events during Eva's interview. You can see Eva's mother looking askance and lowering her voice as she refers to Rosie as a 'girl of low morals'. She begins reluctantly at first, '...so glad Eva would be getting away from certain elements...girls can be worse than boys sometimes...you think boys are the violent ones but that's not always the case, is it?' She offers crafted fragments of information, forcing the headmaster to tease out all the details if only to make sense of what she is saying.

It wasn't *her* idea, she can say later. The headmaster *forced* her to tell.

You can imagine Eva's blow-by-blow description of the fight playing out as if she hasn't rehearsed it with her mother. For some reason you can't picture the father or his role but you are certain that these people would have said and done everything in their considerable power to make Rosie sound like a monster.

Shit.

Four days later a letter from Mount Karver arrives. Still clinging to hope, Rosie dances inside with it, rips open the envelope and scans the letter. Her face falls. She hands the letter to Wendy who scans it and hands it to you.

Rosie has not been accepted in the first round of applications but may be considered in the second round.

You wonder if this is, in fact, true.

Ignatius Quinn is canny enough to realise that if he refused entry to Rosie outright, you would respond with an open declaration of war, bombarding the school board with letters of protest outlining how you have become part of the Mount Karver 'family' via fundraisers, fetes and sporting events—you deserve greater consideration than this.

Ignatius Quinn is cunning enough to dull the pain by turning the rejection into a two-step process. There can be no howls of protest if Rosie still has a chance of being accepted in a second round. Then, once you are acclimatised to the possibility that Rosie may not be offered a place, he deals the final blow.

Wendy takes the letter from your hands and draws your attention to Rosie, who hunches at the kitchen table, staring out the window. There are no histrionics, not even a little weeping.

'Is there anything I can do?' Rosie eventually asks.

'Write a letter,' says Wendy.

Rosie bustles into her room and returns with a pad and paper. You privately wonder whether it isn't cruel to offer your daughter hope. But you don't have the heart to stop her as she starts a letter to Doctor Quinn outlining why she would be a valuable asset to the school and telling him how much she would like to attend. She finishes it in her lovely clean handwriting and passes it to Wendy for proofing.

Rosie has her mother's gift for letter writing. Her plea is passionate and genuine. Despite the fact that it has a few spelling mistakes and some grammatical deviations, Wendy doesn't change a word.

22

When Wendy takes a call from Elsie Schmetterling, she guesses she's getting the inside lowdown on Rosie's letter to Ignatius Quinn. But the call is not about Rosie at all—it's about the gun incident. You overhear enough of Wendy's conversation to be suppressing a wave of panic by the time she hangs up. You discover that the police have requested a meeting in Ignatius Quinn's office with both O'Dell parents, Constable Lance Johnstone, the area commander, and the superintendent in charge of weapons licensing.

Eek. And shit.

According to Elsie, the headmaster has no clue as to their agenda but wants you to attend. Wendy tells Elsie that she'll get back to her.

Wendy calls Shelley Mainwaring but you are interrupting

with so many questions that she hands over the receiver. Shelley recommends that Wendy attend the meeting but not you. This makes you relieved and alarmed.

Relieved because you are a coward and have no wish to attend and now you have a legitimate excuse because you are following legal advice. *Alarmed* because you thought the whole thing had blown over but now your lawyer is advising you not to attend, which indicates that you are still in jeopardy.

You ask whether you are still in jeopardy. Shelley knows you are a headcase so is careful not to inflame you with her answer. Because the police have still not formally responded to the written statement that you submitted shortly after Constable Johnstone threatened to arrest you, Shelley is not satisfied that the matter has been resolved. There is a remote chance (she emphasises *remote*) that the meeting could be some kind of ambush.

'What kind of ambush?'

'They might arrest you.'

A lava of stuttering gibberish erupts out of you so Wendy takes the phone. Wendy can't believe that the cops would try to arrest you when you have done nothing wrong. Shelley reminds Wendy that Constable Lance Johnstone is a loose cannon. Who knows what kind of scenario he has created in the minds of his superiors?

Every time you visit your psychiatrist, he asks you to fill in a form with the same questions:

Do you have nightmares?

Do you try not to think about your accident?

163

Are you always on guard?

Are you easily startled?

Do you feel detached from others?

Are you interested in reading books or magazines?

There's a couple of pages of questions like these. You are supposed to answer *yes* or *no* and then rate the intensity of your feeling out of 10. Today it goes:

Nightmares, yes, 8 (down from 9 last week)

Think of accident, yes, 7 (up from 5)

On guard, yes, 10 (always)

Easily startled, yes, 10 (always)

Detached from others, yes, 9 (same as last week)

Interested in reading, no, 2 (same as last week)

You suppose Doctor Maurice tracks your scores to monitor your progress. *It seems awfully simple. Can you really be summed up with a series of scores? Maybe you can.* On the inside you feel like a complex mass of intertwining disasters but maybe from the outside you're just a Fuck-up Grade B with a degree of difficulty of zero point seven.

Anyway, you like Doctor Maurice (it's only in your head that you call him 'Doctor Maurice'; in real life you call him 'Maurice' mostly but sometimes 'Doctor O'Connell'). You like Doctor Maurice because he makes you feel like you are not alone. And because he is kind.

'I have always depended on the kindness of strangers.' You are suddenly transported back to school where you hear your curly-headed friend, Chris Sepak, quoting Blanche DuBois from some Tennessee Williams play. *Which one? Doesn't matter.* It's a routine Chris does for the gang. He raises his voice to a girlish pitch and nails a perfect Southern accent. 'I have always depended on the kindness of strangers.' You all laugh uproariously.

The doctor asks you why you are smiling and you answer, 'Nothing,' which doesn't exactly make sense. You kick yourself mentally for not paying attention to this man who is trying to help you.

Doctor Maurice scans the form you have just filled in and asks you how you've been going. You tell him about the all-pervasive dread you are experiencing. You know it's not rational but you feel that the *good part of your life is over and the bad part has begun.*

You see that you have been engaged in a ridiculous, new-agey pact with the universe: *I will be a good person and good things will happen to me.* You've been thinking that since your accident the universe hasn't kept up its end of the bargain. But recently you've begun to realise that the universe is, in fact, trying to tell you something: that in your core you are not such a good person. You're not bad. You're just not good *enough.*

Doctor Maurice interrupts, 'Listen to me, Michael. Bad things happen to good people. They do. They just do.'

You know he's just trying to be kind but kindness is the thing that always gets you. You struggle to stop the tears but they come anyway, tumbling down your cheeks, girlish embarrassments like Chris Sepak's high-pitched voice.

Yet again you curse your emotional incontinence. *How the gang at school would laugh.*

As Maurice hands you a tissue you admit that you are

terrified of being arrested; terrified in the way that people are terrified of elevators or heights. The fear may be irrational but it is also limitless and immense.

Doctor Maurice can feel your terror and comes and sits on the couch next to you. Somehow his physical proximity comforts you. 'I am with you,' it says.

You tell him about your godfather who is long dead but was Deputy Commissioner of Police when you were a boy. He was stern, kind and dependable. You held him in the highest possible esteem. Because of him, you grew up believing that the police were there to serve and protect. You always took comfort in their presence. It never occurred to you that they wouldn't be on your side.

How can it be that they have become a sinister shadow looming over everything?

Leaving the psychiatrist's office, you close the glossy fire-engine-red front door and step outside, where you are almost run over by a postman on a bicycle.

You push your way down the narrow sidewalk against a stream of pedestrians. They are all well-dressed, young, vital, filled with purpose and headed to important destinations. Then you see someone out of place like yourself.

An Aboriginal man, about your age, moves slower than the other pedestrians. He watches his feet as he walks, not making eye contact with anyone. The frayed cuffs of his long-sleeved white shirt are turned up a couple of times, just like yours. He wears faded jeans with scuffed Birkenstocks and has an air of peacefulness about him.

When he passes, he glances directly at you. You see that

you have been wrong. The man's eyes are filled with pain, not peace. Nothing is said and he walks on. But you are struck by a profound connection. You feel it in some inner place that you would call a soul if you were convinced such a thing exists.

A question stops you in your tracks: here you are, middle class, white, well educated, well connected, living in fear of the police coming to arrest you. *What must it be like to be poor, black, with little education or opportunity? Where do you turn for comfort and support when the police come after you? How do you assert your rights? Who will help you? What do you do with the certainty of your complete powerlessness? How fucking unbearable must that feel?*

You stumble and put your hand on a parked car to stop yourself falling. Suddenly you feel sick and a stream of vomit erupts from your mouth and splatters into the gutter.

'Hey, that's my car!' a man's voice calls behind you. A small amount of vomit has splashed onto the door of the red car.

A little while later you are sitting in your own car, trying to collect yourself before you attempt to drive home. You wipe your mouth with your handkerchief and put it back in your pocket, where you discover a twenty-dollar bill. It occurs to you that you should go back and give it to the owner of the vomit-specked car, a contribution towards a carwash.

You walk back to find him but he is gone.

23

Lining up at your local cinema, you've bought your (tax-deductible) ticket and are looking forward to the oblivion that is granted when the lights go down and you immerse yourself in someone else's story.

An usher appears and opens one of the double doors to the cinema. As patrons pour out of the previous session, you study their faces; they're smiling and chatting, which is a good sign because it's a comedy.

Suddenly you realise that you've forgotten your pad and special pen that has a tiny light on it so you can take notes in the dark. You will need these notes to compose your review. You pat yourself down to make sure you haven't tucked them into a pocket somewhere, but, no, they're not there.

Idiot.

Maybe you left them in the car.

If you go to the car now you will lose your place in the line which may mean you will miss out on your favourite seat almost exactly in the middle of the cinema—halfway between the screen and the projector, fifteen seats from the left exit, fourteen seats from the right exit.

You hover for a moment, seized by indecision. When the cinema is finally empty the usher opens the second door, allowing patrons to enter for the next session. As the line starts to move, you engage in a panicky dialogue with yourself.

Maybe you can write the review without notes?

What if you can't?

Then you could just see it again.

But what a waste of time and money.

You should have gone to the press screening yesterday instead of mucking around at your psychiatrist's.

Mucking around?

Is that really what you think, you infant?

Why can't you calm down and stop catastrophising?

...Is that even a word?

You peel out of the line and run back to your car. Pad and pen are not on the seat or in the compartment between the front seats. You check the glove box and feel around on the floor. You open the back door and grope under the seats. Nothing.

You must have left them at home. *Shit.*

Out of breath, you sit in the driver's seat, cursing yourself. It does not occur to you that the proprietor of the cinema could lend you a pen and paper. It does not occur to you that you are parked in a shopping centre where any number of shops would happily sell you a pen and paper. It does not occur to you that either of these arrangements could be made well before your movie commences, while the ads and trailers are running.

So you drive home thinking you'll go to an evening session instead, congratulating yourself on another day wasted. When you pull into the driveway mid-afternoon, Wendy's car is there.

Ugly hot panic flushes through you. *Why is she home in the middle of the day? What's gone wrong now?*

Declan comes to the door not wearing his school uniform. *Oh God, he's been expelled.*

'What's happened? Why aren't you at school?'

He narrows his eyes and looks at you as if you are utterly insane. 'It's Saturday,' he answers.

You go inside and there they are—the culprits—the special pen and paper just *sitting there* on the kitchen table in barefaced defiance; *not a care in the world, not a single thought to the trauma they have put you through or the time they have wasted by not being where you thought you had put them.*

Wendy is in the back garden, watering the wilting herb garden that you promised not to neglect but did. She motions for you to come outside, which you do. It's an unusually hot spring day (hence the watering) and Rosie and Juan are splashing around in the pool.

Somewhere in the outer orbits of your consciousness this gives you pleasure because you always suspected that you installed the pool too late for the kids to get proper use out of it.

You grew up with a swimming pool in the days when they were not a common addition to middle-class gardens. You remember your pool as pivotal to your childhood, the centrepiece of long happy summers splashing around with the neighbourhood kids. You loved it until your dad died and money was scarce and the filter pump seemed to break down every second weekend of your adolescence. Then you hated the hours you spent trying to fix it while your mother wept quietly in the kitchen, appearing intermittently with cordial and cake to thank you for being such a good boy.

You didn't want a pool because of these memories but Wendy pushed it and eventually you conceded when Declan was in his final year of primary school. You spent way too much on the construction and ended up having to do the landscaping yourself.

You're particularly proud of the stand of Australian native ferns and palms you planted. They took a couple of years to establish but now provide a handsome screen from the surrounding houses.

Wendy says something with her mouth closed. It sounds like 'rook' but you realise it's 'look'. She cocks her head sideways towards the swimming pool.

You scan the pool area where Rosie and Juan splash each other, oblivious to your presence. You scan the palms to see if one has died. You try to peer beyond the palms into the yard next door.

You look back to Wendy and shrug.

She rolls her eyes and turns her back to the pool so she is directly facing you. The spray of the hose comes with her but she whips it away before it wets you. 'Juan,' she says very quietly. 'Look at Juan.'

You look at Juan, laughing and splashing, and then you see it. You can't quite believe you're seeing it so you position yourself to get a better view. Sure enough, there it is.

You turn to Wendy, your mouth agape.

'Holy shit,' you say, then you both turn back to look at Juan.

Emblazoned across his chest—worse than emblazoned: *tattooed*—in ornate capital letters is the name ROSIE.

'Is that a real tattoo?'

'Apparently.'

'How do you know?'

'He told me.'

'What did he say?'

'I said, "Is that a tattoo?" and he said, "Yes."'

'What did Rosie say?'

'Rosie thinks it's cool.'

'What do we do?'

'What can we do? We're not his parents.'

'Yeah but...'

'Yeah, I know.'

Declan starts his final exams in mid-October. First up is a three-hour English paper. You're glad because English is one of his strong suits and hopefully it will give him the confidence boost he needs to get through the next six examinations, spread out over a gruelling three weeks.

You're in the study when you hear a doof-doof outside

and you look out the window to see Declan pour out of a green sedan packed with Mount Karver boys. It's a hot day—summer has arrived prematurely—and the lads have shed their blazers and ties. There are shouts of farewell and some four-letter banter and the car doof-doofs away.

Declan strolls up the winding front path with a satchel slung over his shoulder, swinging his blazer. There is a lightness to him that might indicate relief that the exam is over or, better still, that he feels he has done well.

He kisses you hello at the door and brightly answers, 'Good!' when you ask him how it went.

Phew!

You follow him into the kitchen and are only a few minutes into the laborious process of trying to extract details from him before the opportunity vanishes, swept away by preparations for the next exam.

He's telling you about the Shakespeare section, and how lucky it was he'd written an essay for Mel on exactly the same topic, when the doorbell rings. You don't want to answer it while you have his attention but it rings again and he goes to see who is there.

Juan's mother, Bernadette, is at your door.

Declan hasn't met Bernadette so she introduces herself and he responds politely and warmly. He explains that Juan is not home but invites her in. She asks where Juan is. He tells her he doesn't know. You can hear the disappointment in her voice and so can Declan so he invites her in again.

You're relieved when you hear her decline. You don't want

to be mean but you want to finish this conversation with your son without interruption.

Then you realise you *are* being mean so you get up and go to the door. 'Hello Bernadette!' you say, with all the enthusiasm you can muster.

Bernadette Moffat sits at your kitchen table, watching Declan kick a soccer ball around the backyard while Egg tries to capture it in his mouth. You look too and register that the lawn needs mowing. Bernadette sips her tea. She tells you what a lovely little boy Juan was until adolescence struck. Her heartbreak is so palpable that you want to give her a hug only you know she'd think it was weird.

She tells you that her daughter Emilia is no trouble at all but Juan has trashed the house so many times that his father refuses to allow him back. He's been in trouble with the police too.

Who hasn't?

Bernadette supposes things would be different if he wasn't adopted. You suggest that kids don't necessarily go bad because they've been adopted. 'Look at Emilia,' you say. 'You just said she was no trouble.'

'Yes, but she's a girl. Girls tend to be more placid.'

Not the ones you know.

You decide to tell Bernadette something you don't tell many people. Not that you keep it a secret but it rarely seems relevant. Right now it is relevant.

'I'm adopted,' you say quietly.

She looks surprised. She asks you how old you were when

you were adopted and you tell her the story: your parents had two natural children, your sisters, Tess and Ingrid. They wanted more but after a series of late-pregnancy miscarriages decided to adopt. You came to them when you were one day old and, even though you've always known you were adopted, your parents embraced you as their son and loved you fiercely. You've always felt like you belonged.

Your sisters never once raised the fact of your adoption, not in argument or even in the subtle devious ways that children can sometimes deploy when there are territorial tussles over toys or belongings or privacy. You never buy lottery tickets because you believe you used up all your luck being chosen by such an extraordinarily accepting family.

Bernadette says most people don't appreciate their families. She tells you how she and her husband John tried and failed with IVF and finally adopted Juan and Emilia from an orphanage in Buenos Aires when he was fifteen months old and she was just over two. It's easier to get them when they are a little bit older and you're prepared to take siblings. She asks you if you know anything about your birth parents but instead of waiting for an answer she tells you that she knows nothing of Juan and Emilia's father, except that he was 'obviously the black one', and little of his mother, except that she was a 'native' living in terrible poverty.

Bernadette doesn't understand why Juan isn't more grateful. He could be stuck in Argentina, starving and penniless. She tells you how they built part of their house as a kind of child's wonderland especially for him and his sister. Emilia appreciates all the opportunities she has been given but Juan just doesn't seem to care. As she begins to list all the things they have bought for him, from skateboards to trail bikes and beyond, you see that she and her husband expect Juan to express his gratitude by being compliant and well behaved.

You imagine his early years when he *was* compliant and well behaved but that wasn't good enough. Back then he was probably supposed to express his gratitude by excelling at everything—best at spelling, best at kicking, best at singing—or by doing as well as Emilia. Emilia won the spelling bee, scored the winning goal, sang the solo. Why didn't you?

You imagine little Juan wilting under the pressure of it all, disappointing them with small failures at first until eventually he thinks, *fuck it I'm not going to play this game.* Then of course it's a slippery slope to smashing up his room and telling his dad to shove his disapproval where the sun don't shine.

It all plays out in front of you until it occurs to you that you do not have sufficient evidence to be so judgmental. Nonetheless, you do feel the burden of Juan's responsibility to be grateful so you point out that Juan doesn't know any different. He's grown up in his luxurious surroundings—that's his reality—not the grinding poverty of his birth mother's world.

Bernadette supposes you're right. And anyway, she adds, kids shouldn't have to be grateful to their parents. It's the parent's job to provide them with everything they can. Right?

Right.

You sip your tea.

'Of course, he was the product of a rape.'

'Pardon?'

'His mother was raped. By her husband but still it was a

rape. That's how she conceived him. Emilia was a different story but that's how she conceived Juan.'

You're taken aback. Why has she given you this information? What are you supposed to do with it? *Does she think her son is the bad seed of an evil action, destined to play out his fate as a bad man?* In some weird way it seems disloyal to have divulged this supposedly damning fact.

'Do you think—?' you begin to ask.

'Well, is it nature or nurture? That's all I'm saying.'

'So you think he's somehow programmed?'

'I wouldn't go that far. I just sometimes think that, no matter what I do, I'm up against it. That's all.'

You're not sure why but there's something in this idea that you find deeply offensive. You feel a sudden well of protective affection for the kid living in the converted garage under your house. You know you have no right to judge this woman— God knows, you're stumbling through parenthood pretty pitifully yourself—but you feel compelled to say, 'Well, he's always welcome here.'

'You haven't seen the horrible side of him. Not yet, anyway.'

You are suddenly reminded of your own mother asking you, aged fifteen, after a terrible fight about not being allowed out when all your friends were, why you were so nice to everybody else and so horrible to her. 'But you're my mother!' you replied, as if that made her the natural repository of all your ills and woes. You recall the way she looked at you, still reeling from the crossfire of harsh words, but so deeply satisfied with your answer that you thought she might crow.

You look at Juan's mother and wonder whether to tell her about her son's new tattoo. You decide not to because:

(a) she'll find out soon enough, and

(b) right now she's filled to capacity with doom and gloom.

It wouldn't be like adding another straw to break the camel's back. It would be like dropping a steel girder on the camel from a great height.

24

You've come so often to the psychiatrist's office that his receptionist calls you Mike and you call her Em. This must mean you are pretty close because even Wendy still calls you Michael. Em is in her early thirties and saving to go travelling in Europe with her boyfriend, Anton. Anton still lives at home with his parents and Em is trying to lever him out of his comfort zone.

Em tells you all this stuff and more, much more, while you are pretending to read the glossy magazines that are actually *in*-date in the waiting room. You know all about Em's life, Anton's life, her mum, Jen, her sister, Anna, her previous boss, Derek-the-dentist (she was a dental nurse until boredom struck and she decided to explore psychiatry, quote unquote) and a whole host of other friends and family. Sometimes you have to wait up to twenty minutes to see Doctor Maurice. You can learn a lot about a person in twenty minutes.

You don't like to be rude and tell Em to shut up and download her shit on some other sucker because you don't like to be rude. *Also because she might switch your prescription with a menopausal madwoman's and suddenly you'll be growing man-boobs.* You were almost fifteen kilos overweight at your most recent weigh-in. Man-boobs are the last thing you need.

This week Doctor Maurice wants to explore previous traumatic events in your life. He tried to do this before but you've always baulked at the idea, essentially because you feel your cup runneth over with current traumas. But Doctor Maurice persists, insisting that it is essential to your recovery. He thinks the trauma of the accident has triggered the memory of previous traumas, and because you have not resolved your feelings about them you are unable to move on and deal with this one. There's a logic to it, you suppose, so you consent to go 'exploring' with him.

First stop is your adoption. He has tried to go here before but you think it's a mistake. You do not think of your adoption as a trauma. Quite the opposite: you think of it as a magnificent piece of luck. You point out that you are not the only one who feels lucky to be part of your family. You have discussed this with both of your sisters on a number of occasions; you all feel the great good fortune of being parented by your particular parents. Your mother has been dead for three years, your father has been dead for thirty. But you can still feel their love raining down on you every day. What can possibly be traumatic about that?

You suddenly realise that you are raising your voice at Doctor Maurice but you're glad so you don't apologise.

He gives you a tight little smile and presses on. 'That's all true but the fact remains that your birth mother abandoned you.'

'She didn't abandon me. She gave me to a good family because she wasn't in a position to take care of me herself.'

'Sorry, I'm not suggesting any negligence on her part or that it wasn't the right thing to do. It was an incredibly courageous thing to do. But the fact remains that there was a point at which you were left. After your birth mother gave you up and before your mother collected you.'

Oh sure. Blah blah blah. The whole discussion has just become way too look-at-me-I'm-an-abandoned-orphan for words. Even with your grand capacity for self-indulgence, you can't go there. You tell him he's off-course and it's wasting your time. You ask him to move on or end the session early. It's your first tiff and you win. You move on to your father's death, which actually *was* traumatic, although what that has to do with falling apart after being run over by a car you're not sure.

Juan's father relents and decides to allow Juan to come home, where the glittering fat-tyred Ford awaits in the six-car garage by the harbour. Juan finds you in the study and comes to tell you and thank you for having him. He's very formal and shakes your hand and you give him a sort of half-hug. You wish him the best and tell him it has been a pleasure having him. You want to say more but the appropriate tone evades you and Juan terminates the exchange by thanking you very formally again and backing out of the study.

In all the months that he has lived downstairs, you've never once glimpsed the real boy beyond his wall of fearful politeness. You've never glimpsed the demons his mother has told you about. You want to go after him and tell him that he's a good boy, that it's okay to be flawed, that his future is in his own hands. But you don't.

Someone comes to pick Juan up. Bernadette, you presume. She doesn't come in. She just honks the horn and Juan runs off down the path with a small backpack of belongings. Rosie waves from the front porch. When she comes inside you ask her how she feels.

'Relieved,' she says.

You ruminate over her answer as she goes into the kitchen and makes a chocolate milk. Have you been doing her any favours, allowing her boyfriend to live downstairs for so many months? Did taking the boy into your home merely enable him to disconnect from his family, leaving his girlfriend— your daughter—as his only real go-to person? And isn't that a huge responsibility for any fourteen-year-old?

No wonder she's relieved. You idiot.

Finally you get a small break with your book. An influential director agrees to an interview. This is important because other directors will follow and once you have a few key directors the movie stars will follow too. You've had a limited response to your grovelling letters via managers and publicists but you hope that this interview might be the tipping point.

You agree to meet in a local café, which you choose, a fair schlep from the beachfront home where the director lives but apparently close to his mum's house where he grew up. He's having dinner with his elderly mum and will 'swing by' the café for a couple of hours beforehand.

It all sounds wonderfully casual until you're waiting for him to arrive in the café and realise how horribly ordinary it is. It's spotlessly clean and unambiguously bourgeois. Clearly nothing interesting has ever happened in this café. It's not funky or bohemian or quirky. Someone may have died here, of boredom, but that is all. *Why did you suggest here of all places?*

You are seized by the idea that your boring choice of venue will reflect poorly on you and your book. Boring Michael O'Dell and his boring book. You remind yourself that the director has grown up in the area, that he will be expecting the kind of place where a decaf café latte is still regarded as slightly exotic, which is exactly what this place is. You calm yourself by checking your pad and pen and spare pen; all working. You make a prat of yourself by speaking into the mic of your small digital recorder. 'Testing, testing.' You play it back. 'Testing, testing,' a tinny voice says back to you. *All good.*

The director arrives, disconcertingly accompanied by an attractive young woman whom he introduces without elaboration as Dana. Dana explains that she's his PA and not to mind her—she'll just sit over there. Dana sits two tables away and you begin the interview.

Despite the fact that he is wearing rock-star sunglasses, the thing that strikes you about this guy is his flesh-on-bone humanity. He's just a person who can't believe how lucky he is that he gets to direct movies for a living. You share a laugh about his uncomplicated middle-class roots and his lack of appropriate artistic angst. Chatting about the nearby suburb where he grew up, he riffs poetically about rampaging through the bush as a kid, roaming free in a world where he could disappear on a bike after breakfast and stay out till dinnertime without a single soul checking where he was.

It's all perfectly innocuous but you feel this cold sweat creeping across your skin. You excuse yourself and go to the bathroom where you give your bloated reflection a stern talking-to. Everything depends on this—not just the book but also your career, your financial future, your house, your kids' education (well, Rosie's anyway), and probably your marriage. You cannot expect Wendy to carry the load as she has been doing.

It's time to get with the program, answer the call to arms, step up to the plate.

What the fuck are you doing?

You splash cold water on your face and feel your heart beating in your chest so fast that you think you might be having a heart attack.

It's not a heart attack. It's a panic attack. Calm down. That's all you have to do.

You look in the mirror. Your usually pink Celtic complexion is a strange greeny-white. *Maybe it's the fluorescent light.* You look at the ceiling; *nup, no fluorescent light.*

Splash more water on your face! your inner voice shouts at you, so you splash more water on your face. You check the mirror again and all the colours fade from your vision and you're looking at yourself in black and white. You notice a funny kind of whooshing feeling from the top of your head as the blood seems to drain from your brain. You realise you are going to faint so you sit on the tiled floor and then lie down so that your face touches the cool tiles.

The cool tiles feel wonderfully soothing. *Wonderfully.* You close your eyes, just for a minute.

The next thing you know Dana is shaking you gently by your shoulder. You open your eyes.

Oh, the horror, the horror.

Your shirt has risen up over your belly and you pull it back down to conceal the roll of fat bulging over the waistband of your too-tight jeans. You sit up and quickly make up a story that you must be getting the flu. You tell her you're okay now and please not to tell her boss—you'd really appreciate it if you could just go back out and get on with the interview. You ask her what the time is and whether you've been gone long. As if to answer this question the director pops his head around the door to see if everything is okay.

Great. Let's all have a party in the bathroom, shall we?

He helps you to your feet and has you sitting back down at the table in no time. He orders a glass of iced water and insists that Dana drop you home—you can easily reschedule the interview for another time, he says. You know this last part is not true because in two days he is leaving for Los Angeles where he will be shooting a film for the better part of a year. You try to protest and assure him that you're okay to continue but in your heart you know you have fucked this up. He says, smiling warmly, that you are clearly unwell and terminates the interview. For a moment you consider whether you should just beg for a second chance but decide against it, not because you are too proud, but because it's poor strategy to sound that desperate.

Dana carries your pad, pens and tape recorder to her car while you shuffle behind her like an invalid. The director farewells you in the car park and tells you to take care of yourself. By the time Dana has driven you the five minutes down the hill back to your house, you hate yourself deeply.

You stagger in the door and Wendy calls chirpily from the kitchen, 'You're back early. How did it go?'

You walk into the kitchen and she takes one look at you and says flatly, 'Oh my God, you're green.'

'It didn't go too well,' you say.

'Oh bummer,' she says, as if you've just told her you spilled a drop of coffee on your white shirt. She kisses you on the cheek and heads towards the door, all dressed up in a sharp suit and stilettos.

'Where are you going?' you call after her.

'That thing at the school,' she calls back and you hear the front door slam.

What thing at the school? you ask yourself.

And then you remember.

After weeks of negotiations and at least three cancellations, Wendy is going to Mount Karver for the meeting in the headmaster's office to 'discuss' the gun incident with the cops and Ignatius Quinn.

And that's why she has breezed out the door: to convince

you that there's nothing to worry about even though you know she is probably shitting bricks of worry right now.

Your wife is a hero and you know that you should stop and give thanks but all you feel is shame. Shame and anxiety. Oh, you're anxious all right. You're plenty anxious. You're *an anxiety-ridden-self-indulgent-useless-no-good-piece-of-worthless-shit-weak-as-piss-pussy.*

25

The traffic is unusually heavy for this time of evening, making Wendy ten minutes late by the time she swings into the Mount Karver gates, kicking herself because she wanted to have some time alone with the headmaster before the police arrived. To make matters worse, there's a Parents and Friends fundraiser on and every available park in the school grounds is taken. Except for a spot with a sign saying, 'Reserved for School Matron.'

The matron runs the school infirmary with the compassionless efficiency you'd expect from Adolf Hitler's sister. She and Wendy detest each other, ever since a row about Declan being sent back to class after breaking two ribs in Year 7. It gives Wendy no small amount of pleasure to pull the car into the matron's space thinking, *Just you try me, Bitch Face.*

Wendy works up a light sweat hurrying to the imposing administration building and is slightly out of breath by the time Elsie Schmetterling greets her at the door to the outer office, waving her inside and whispering, 'They're all in there! They're all in there!' Wendy ducks into the ladies, checks her makeup and pats her perspiration down with some light powder. She returns, looking composed and formidable despite the fact that she is a bundle of nerves.

Elsie swings open the door to the headmaster's office and clears her throat. Wendy enters and begins the long walk across the Persian carpets, allowing three policemen in different uniforms to study her.

They see a woman striding towards them in a tailored grey suit and some snappy red heels. Wendy feels the frisson she has created entering a room full of men and makes a mental note to use this to her advantage.

The headmaster stands and says, 'Mrs O'Dell,' rather than 'Ms Weinstein'. Wendy doesn't bother to correct him. She shakes his hand and he makes the introductions. Wendy does not extend her hand to the others; she nods at each, restraining her natural warmth. If you were in the room right now it would occur to you that your wife is looking incredibly sexy.

Constable Lance Johnstone makes a stupid joke about having met her before, which she ignores. He is scrubbed and polished within an inch of his life, wearing his best uniform, but there is still something third-rate about him.

Superintendent Dieter Margan has a bald head and lots of shiny bits on his dark blue uniform. His manner and demeanour remind Wendy of Yul Brynner during his *King and I* days.

The third guy is also in uniform. She doesn't catch his rank but the headmaster explains that the darkly handsome Tony Haddad is in charge of gun licensing.

Wendy sits in a wingback chair and crosses her legs. 'So how can I help you gentlemen?' she says like she's a character in a Bond movie.

After some brief umming and ahing, Ignatius Quinn explains that the superintendent has asked for an assurance that the police will be forewarned the next time a student undertakes any activity involving a replica firearm.

'But now that we all know it's illegal, the students won't be using replica firearms,' says Wendy, feigning restrained astonishment, 'will they, Doctor Quinn?'

'Quite right, Mrs O'Dell.'

'Declan didn't know he was using an illegal firearm, otherwise he wouldn't have borrowed it. It was an innocent mistake, that's all.'

'But what about your husband, Mrs O'Dell?' says Dieter Margan. 'Surely he would have realised that it was a replica Glock?'

Wendy looks baffled. 'I'm sorry. Are you asking me whether Michael knew the toy gun was illegal?' She calls it a *toy gun* rather than a *replica Glock* to provoke a response.

It works.

'Toy gun? Toy gun?' splutters Lance Johnstone. The superintendent shoots a look that tells him to shut up but Lance doesn't take the cue. 'It's hardly a toy gun.'

'Well, I understand it fires potato pellets. Is that correct?'

'Yes, Mrs O'Dell, it—'

'Has anybody ever been killed by a potato pellet?' interrupts Wendy.

'It might take out your eye!' declares Lance Johnstone.

'Yes. If it had potato pellets in it. Did the gun have potato pellets in it when you confiscated it, Constable?'

'Not at the time, no but—'

'Then it was a harmless toy gun.'

'Harmless? It wasn't harmless! It's a replica of a deadly weapon. A deadly weapon. You don't seem to appreciate, Mrs O'Dell, that I would have shot the boy holding that gun. I would have shot the boy holding that gun!'

And off he goes, just like he did that day outside the canteen. He launches into a rant, repeating the same stupid declaration. When Dieter Margan and Tony Haddad exchange a look, Wendy relaxes. She sees that they can see what a complete lunatic Constable Lance Johnstone really is.

The headmaster stops the constable mid-stream. 'Just hold on a minute, Constable. If you had shot the boy you saw holding that gun, neither you nor I would be here. I would have resigned for allowing a boy to be killed on my watch. And you would be facing manslaughter charges.'

'Quite right, Headmaster,' chimes in the superintendent, 'quite right.'

Lance Johnstone looks around the room bewildered, wondering what he has done wrong. His superiors hurriedly wrap up the meeting and bundle him out of the room. As they beat a retreat across the Persian carpets, Wendy inquires whether they are still considering arresting you.

Superintendent Dieter Margan looks back at her, astonished. 'Arrest your husband?'

'Yes.'

'We never intended to.'

'So he's safe?'

'Of course he's safe.'

And so they leave.

Wendy turns to the headmaster who grins. He's too discreet to say anything but she can tell he thinks they were a bunch of tossers.

'What do you think will happen to Constable Johnstone?' she asks.

'I imagine he's being rigorously counselled this very minute,' says the headmaster.

There is a knock at the door. Elsie is standing there with an *uh-oh* look on her face, next to Matron Hitler. Wendy has lost a few kilos since their last interaction but the matron appears to have found them; her large bosom strains against the buttons of her crisp white uniform.

'We think Mrs O'Dell may have parked in Matron's spot,' offers Elsie as Matron looks on in wordless disapproval.

'Yes I have,' says Wendy brightly, making no apology and no effort whatsoever to get up and right the wrong, 'I have indeed!'

Back at home you know none of this. You have no idea that the meeting is over or that Matron Hitler has exacted her revenge by parking Wendy in and vanishing into the maze of school buildings, leaving her stranded and ruing her decision to linger longer than necessary in the headmaster's office.

All you know is that your poor wife is up at the school, once again fighting your battles for you. You are in such a state of anxiety pacing around the house that you decide to pace outside in the garden to see if that will help.

It doesn't.

You decide to go for a walk around the block and head back inside to ask Egg if he wants to come too, but he barely raises his head from the doggy bed so you go by yourself. The light is fading fast but instead of making a left turn at the end of the street, you head down a laneway between two wooden bungalows and into the untamed bushland behind them.

Normally the bush soothes you, particularly at dusk, but right now your mind races, spiralling into disastrous scenarios: Wendy being arrested instead of you; Wendy escaping the cops but being run over by a car; Wendy escaping but shooting Lance Johnstone and being re-arrested; Wendy escaping but being shot by Lance Johnstone; you telling your children that their mother has been shot.

As you stumble down the stony track, an idea forms and sets like concrete: *Wendy and the kids would be better off without you.*

You have nothing to offer them. You are nothing but a drain on their resources. You remember your life insurance policy and realise that if you died, Wendy would be able to pay off the mortgage. Without the mortgage payments, Wendy and the kids could easily survive on her wage. There's a clause that invalidates the policy in case of suicide but a fall out here in the bush could easily look like an accident.

Wendy and the kids would be better off without you.

You have left no suicide note. There would be nothing to indicate that a fall was anything but a horrible accident. A man with the flu, a little feverish and disoriented, goes wandering in the bush at the end of his street and falls off a cliff. Simple. You end the humiliating failure of your life and Wendy and the kids can live worry-free. It makes such sense.

Wendy and the kids would be better off without you.

You take the right fork in the track. A wattle branch whips you in the face but you hardly feel it. You know what to do now. Soon you reach a small sandstone cliff. You stand on the edge and look down. It's not very high—only about ten metres—but if you land head-first on the rock platform below your neck should break.

Wendy and the kids would be better off without you.

Come on. You can do this. It's like diving into a pool. Easy. You take a few steps back, as if you're going for a dive. You don't want to get up too much speed and leap out too far because it won't look like an accident. And you must remember to keep your hands by your sides because they might break the fall. You don't want to survive this and end up in a wheelchair, yet another burden for Wendy to deal with.

Wendy and the kids would be better off without you.

You've forgotten to count how many paces it is to the edge. You pace it out. One, two, three…and a half and you are looking over the edge again. *Hmm. A half is no good.* Better to pace backwards, counting so you know exactly when your foot will step into air. *And which foot?* Your left, you decide.

You take a step back, beginning with your left foot, and start to count back from five.

Your foot slips in a spray of sandy pebbles. Your leg slides from under you and you lurch forward to right yourself. You lurch over the cliff. And then, because you are running purely on instinct, you pull back, arms outstretched, regaining your balance just in time to stop yourself toppling off the edge. It makes no difference whether you go over now or in a few moments. In fact, it's better to go now when it actually is an accident. But it's too late; you've saved yourself. You're going to have to do it with intent.

Shit. You feel the adrenaline pumping through your body. You can do this.

You are doing this.

And as soon as you have surrendered to the certainty of this idea, a flood of relief washes over you. You have a plan. You are going to enact the plan.

You are doing this.

To make sure that you don't slip again, you crouch and brush away the sand and pebbles in your path. Under the pebbles, someone has scratched some letters into the rock. It's almost dark now so it's hard to read but you see the word, ZORBA.

Nothing else, just ZORBA.

That's pretty weird because Zorba is your man and *Zorba the Greek* is your touchstone book. *Maybe the universe is trying to tell you something…*

Oh God, here you go again! Stop with the childlike yearning. Stop apportioning meaning to events that have none. The universe is not trying to communicate with you or anyone else! It just IS, for fuck's sake.

It's a small riff of irritation but it breaks the spell.

It suddenly strikes you that killing yourself is a really stupid idea. And now it's not Zorba but Anna Karenina who comes to you. As she hurls herself under the wheels of the train, Anna wonders what on earth she is doing. She feels silly. And that's what you feel. *Silly.* Nothing grand or profound— just your ordinary old garden-variety *silly.*

You sit on your bum and look around you. A full moon rises and the bush comes alive. Ringtail possums wake in the eucalypts towering above. A riot of kookaburras chortle their last hurrah for the evening. Crickets and frogs chirp and croak and bonk an almost deafening symphony. You get to your feet, brush the sand from your jeans, and head back down the track.

In ten minutes you emerge from the laneway between the two wooden bungalows and are in your street with the lights buzzing over your head. You walk up over the rise and see your house in the dip beyond, peeking though the greenery of your rambling garden. The lights are on, which means someone is home.

26

Doctor Maurice O'Connell wears a red shirt with yellow stripes. There is something perkily optimistic about those bright stripes that shames you into silence. You can't bring yourself to tell him about your recent escapades in the bush. You feel you've let him down and you don't want to let him down today. Especially when he is wearing his happy shirt.

No, tell him, you doofus, that's what he's there for.

But you can't.

Your pathetic brush with suicide is too ridiculous to confess to another person, even if he is a professional trying to salvage your mental health. You couldn't tell Wendy either, after she came home from Mount Karver. Brimming with good news, she looked so relieved that you couldn't bear to dish up more shit when she had just cleared her plate. Maybe it wasn't honest but sometimes honesty is overrated.

You're weighing up the ethics of your decision when the good doctor zeros in on your inner turmoil and starts prodding. You don't give him much so he goes to that reliable place where he knows he can get a rise out of you: your adoption. Or rather, his take on your adoption.

Here we go again.

Only this time it is different. This time he connects the dots. He leads you back through your accident and your notion that the universe had abandoned your contract with it. From there he takes you back to your mother's death; a kind of abandonment. Declan's birth during which he almost dies, almost abandoning you. Your best friend from university, Dazza, dies in your arms after a car accident; another kind of abandonment. A teacher doesn't believe your pain and abandons you in the locker room where you almost die of a ruptured appendix. Non-malignant tumours on both your ears grow so large that your hearing abandons you for six weeks before they are removed. Your father's death: just when you are on the threshold of manhood, you experience another kind of abandonment.

Is it not possible that you have been unable to process what happened to you with the car accident because you have not acknowledged the full effect of these previous traumas? And is it not possible that you have not processed these previous traumas because you have not processed the original trauma—your adoption?

'I really think you need to acknowledge that you were abandoned as a baby. Don't attach to it, don't get stuck to it, just walk around it and say, "That happened".'

'Look. Maurice. I really appreciate that you are trying to help me. But I have to tell you this problem with my adoption is yours, not mine. I really don't feel like I was...'

And, precisely at that moment, your body hijacks you. You want to say the word *abandoned*. You want to say *I really don't feel like I was abandoned* but you can't. You physically *can't*. Your voice box shuts down. A vacuum forms in your windpipe and you can't get a breath. Your diaphragm contracts and you gasp in air then immediately expel it as a huge sob.

A great, shuddering sob.

The sob sits there in the room between you and Doctor Maurice. He smiles compassionately and says gently, 'There we go,' although you know what he really wants to say is, 'At last.'

You sit in the reverberating shock waves of your single sob. You had no warning it was coming or any idea that you felt this way. It begins to sink in: you *do* feel abandoned. Or did. Whether you have any right to or not, *you do feel like this*. Your mind refused to acknowledge it so your body took control and insisted that you make your feelings known to yourself. It seems an astonishing physical feat.

'Does that happen often?' you ask Doctor Maurice.

'No,' he says. 'Not often.'

27

I'm four and a half years old and playing in front of my house with my neighbours, Molly and Davie, and the boy across the road who is older and has a two-wheel bike that he can ride all by himself. This morning it was so hot that Mr Taylor said you could fry an egg on the road so we tried it with an egg from the Hendricks' chook shed and guess what? You could! Except the yellow doesn't go very hard. Molly and Davie's dog, Robbie, ate most of it even though it was stuck to the road. Anyway right now we're playing under the sprinkler with our clothes on and they're all wet but that's okay because our mums said we could.

The boy across the road with the two-wheeler asks Molly if she knows where babies come from and she says she does and I say that I came from somewhere different because I'm adopted. Davie says, 'You are not,' and I say, 'I am too.' And he says, 'You are not,' and Molly says I'm making it up to show off and I say, 'I am not. Ask Mum.'

So we're going inside to ask Mum.

Mum is cross because we're dripping on the carpet and bringing dirt in so we go out onto the porch.

Molly says, 'Mrs O'Dell, Michael says he's adopted.'

Mum looks at me and then she looks at Molly and says, 'Michael makes things up.'

And then Davie says, 'Told ya!' and they all go back to the sprinkler.

I stay on the porch with Mum and I'm very angry because I didn't make it up; it's true. Mum says quietly, 'Come inside,' and we go inside to the kitchen even though I leave wet marks on the carpet.

I'm very angry so I kind of shout and cry all at the same time. 'Why did you say that? Why did you say that?' And Mum says, 'I'm sorry my darling,' and gets down on her knees and hugs me so tight I have to squeeze my face free to get a breath and I can tell by the noises she is making that she is crying. And then she looks at me with tears in her eyes and she holds me by the shoulders and says, 'You mustn't tell anyone about that. You must not tell anyone that you're adopted.'

I don't understand why she is so upset so I ask why I can't tell anyone and she says it's because they won't understand. She says that I belong to Dad and her and Tess and Ingrid. She says we all belong together and it doesn't matter who's adopted and who's not. But people won't understand if I tell them I'm adopted. They'll treat me like I'm different and I'm not different.

I don't really understand what she is saying but I do understand I must not tell anyone I'm adopted. Mum asks me to promise so I promise. Molly and Davie knock on the door and ask if I'm coming back out to play and Mum smiles and pretends she hasn't been crying and says, 'Yes, he'll be out in a minute.' And then she gets ice-blocks out of the freezer and I choose a red one and take the rest out to the other kids and we all play in the sprinkler again.

I'm twenty years old, in the second year of university, and life is pretty damn fine. I've just broken up with my second long-term girlfriend and I've decided to play the field for a while. I've made a decision not to settle down until I'm about thirty. That gives me ten good years of partying, after which I'll need a rest anyway. That's my life plan. I like my plan. It's a good plan.

Sitting next to me in the Linguistics 235 tutorial is my mate Dazza. He likes my plan too. He likes it so much that he's decided to use it as his life plan as well.

The tutor asks a question and a voice answers. I can't explain this but the voice is incredibly familiar even though I haven't heard it before. It belongs to a girl I haven't even seen but I know instantly that she is *important*. A voice within me says *Oh, so there she is*. I can't see her because we are both sitting on the same side of the long tutorial table with about five or six people between us. I lean forward with no small amount of trepidation and look down the table. I still can't see her because Dazza's big boofy head is in the way so I whisper, 'Hey Dazza, what does she look like?' Dazza has a really long gawp and turns back and says, 'Good.'

Her name is Wendy Weinstein. She is Jewish. Or Jewish-lite as she likes to say. She's the second Jewish person I have encountered. The first was a guy I went to school with but he was kind of annoying so I avoided him.

Within a week of hearing her voice, I tell Wendy I am adopted. She is the only person I have told since I was four and a half years old. I tell Wendy because I sense that we are going down a long road together and it's important not to start off with any secrets.

I am thirty-five years old, standing at the letterbox, flicking through the mail. Electricity bill. *Yay.* Gas bill. *Yippee.* Letter from the hospital where our kids were born. Addressed to me, not me and Wendy. *Odd.* I rip it open and scan. It's not about the kids. It's about me.

The hospital has something called a 'post-adoption agency' and they've recently been contacted by my birth mother. *My birth mother.*

I have a birth mother and she is alive.

I go inside and read the letter with Wendy. My birth mother wants to contact me. She wants to write me a letter. The agency wants to know if I will accept the letter. It's up to me. I just have to say *no* and the matter will be dropped and I won't be contacted again.

Wendy tells me I've gone white. I suddenly feel incredibly tired, overwhelmingly exhausted. It's only four o'clock in the afternoon but I lie down on the bed and fall instantly asleep. I stay asleep until three o'clock the next afternoon, unconscious for twenty-three hours while the known universe shifts slightly to the left.

I tell my mother about the letter from my birth mother and her eyes well with tears. She tells me that she feels like she entered an unspoken contract with my birth mother to raise me as her son and that my birth mother has come back and broken the contract. I put my arms around her while she cries quietly into my shoulder.

I tell her if it's going to cause her so much pain, I won't proceed. The tears dry up and she tells me not to be ridiculous. Just because she doesn't want it doesn't mean I shouldn't want it. She tells me she's always been amazed by my lack of curiosity. I tell her that I am curious but I've never felt the need to go looking for my birth parents. This must be because I have such great parents. Her eyes well with tears again but this time she gets that look like she might crow.

I'm twenty-six years old, holding my day-old son. Light pours through the old Georgian windows of Wendy's hospital room in the neo-natal unit. I look up and see my mother studying me from a chair in the corner.

'What?' I say, smiling.

'That's your own flesh and blood,' she says. 'That's the first time you've held your own flesh and blood.'

I look back in wonder at my boy. She's right. He is the only person I have ever met who comes from the same gene pool. And what is remarkable to me about that fact is that it's not important. *He's here. He's himself. That's the important bit. He is here to be loved and I love him.* I glimpse for a moment how my own parents embraced me instantly and completely even though I am not their biological child.

I am thirty-six years old, meeting my birth mother for the first time. We've corresponded for eighteen months and now we are face to face. We sit in the modest kitchen of her home, a four-hour flight north of mine. She speaks softly, a quiet, self-contained sort of person.

There is something incredibly dear about her.

As she lifts her teacup to her mouth, we are simultaneously conscious that her hand is trembling. I feel an immense gratitude for the gift of life she has given me. She tries to master the tremble but her hand shakes harder and she is forced to put her cup back in the saucer.

This isn't going to be easy.

I'm forty-one years old and my mother is dying. We both know it. I sit at her bedside in the nursing home, holding her hand.

When did those hands get so bony? So blue-veined and flesh-less?

I remember being a little boy, no more than three or four, and our positions are reversed. I am in bed and she is holding my hand. I have woken with a night terror and she has come to comfort me. I drop off to sleep but wake again in fright. Each time I wake, she is there, holding my hand.

What a privilege it is to be here, holding hers now.

I know she is afraid but she will not tell me because it is her job to comfort me, to stop me from being afraid, not the other way around; this is how she thinks. I brace myself for the hour that she tells me, finally, that she is afraid.

I will know then that the end is very near.

She asks me to close the venetians, which I do. Her once-lively interest in the world contracts on an almost hourly basis. Just a few weeks ago the clock-radio on her pink laminate bedside table would have been barking a political debate. Mum, eyebrows knit in concentration, would offer observations of such pithy accuracy that they took your breath away.

So sharp, this woman, a spitfire all her life but now she is leaving. Receding, not so gradually. Her world has shrunk into a single room where she lies dying. She is only interested in what is going on in the room. It's all about the room. This nurse coming. That nurse going. How much apple juice is left.

She turns and holds me with her watery gaze. There is such love in her look that I can hardly bear it.

'I'm glad she's here,' says my mother.

'Who?'

'Up north,' she answers and I realise she means my birth mother. I take a deep breath to stop myself from bawling. All I can manage is, 'Oh Mamma.'

It occurs to me that I will not know such fierce unconditional love again. I have not yet learned that it will not die with her; that it will travel with me all my days.

28

You are sitting on the couch, cross-legged, attempting the lotus position. Your knees ache and there's a weird twinge in your left hip but you are doing your best to meditate as instructed by Doctor Maurice. You are trying to observe (not attach to!) your feelings of abandonment when Wendy comes through the door with the shopping so you unfold yourself and help her unload the car.

After you've unpacked the groceries together, Wendy says she needs to talk to you about finances. You nod but for some reason you do not feel the usual rush of dread. The loan from Ingrid has helped through the last months but the money is running out again. You're back to the old discussion about generating more income or selling the house. At least you no longer have Declan's school fees to worry about.

You tell Wendy about a phone message from the Rat-tat-tat editor at the *Herald*, the guy who talks without pronouns. You're not exactly sure what he wants but he has asked you to lunch at a fairly swanky restaurant in the city. You are now officially the last person on earth to leap to optimistic conclusions, but you're guessing it could be about writing for a movie website that the paper is launching. You'll also try to step up the freelance work and failing that, the local grocery store is looking for night stackers again.

Wendy takes your hand and strokes it.

'How are you?' she asks.

'A bit better, getting better.'

'Yeah, I can tell.'

'Sorry I've been so useless.'

'It's been pretty horrible, hasn't it?'

You lift her hand and kiss it. 'Thanks for sticking with me.'

She shrugs and gives you a crooked smile.

'Why do you?' you ask. 'Why do you stick with me?'

'You'll come back,' she says, 'and I'll be here.'

Another letter comes from Mount Karver addressed to Rosie. This time there is no joyful dancing, only quiet trepidation. You and Wendy watch your daughter read her letter. She looks puzzled and then her mouth curls into a smile.

'I've got a second interview!' she declares.

Wendy can't make the interview because she is about to leave on a two-day conference. She asks Rosie if she wants to try and move the interview day but Rosie says, 'No, Dad can take me, can't you, Dad?'

You nod manfully but privately baulk at the thought of managing her terrible disappointment if it all goes pear-shaped *which, let's face it, it probably will.*

Two days later you are back in the school's administration building, waiting in the long corridor and not in the anteroom to the headmaster's office. Elsie Schmetterling offers no explanation why she has placed you here. You interpret this as a bad sign.

Elsie reappears and says, 'She'll see you now.'

She?

Rosie shoots you a look as you head south down the corridor instead of north towards the headmaster's office.

'Where are we going?' you ask.

'The deputy's office,' answers Elsie, like it's the most natural thing in the world.

A sense of doom sinks like a lead weight in your gut. You were hoping that Wendy's session with the headmaster might have improved his disposition towards Rosie. But the gutless turd is getting his deputy, Sabina Smith, to do his dirty work for him.

Sabina Smith is a sturdily built woman with a mean face that belies a kind and friendly spirit. She's the ideal person to inform Rosie of her rejection, and negotiate her way through parental outrage on the school's behalf.

Ms Smith's office is almost hilariously austere compared to the splendour of Ignatius Quinn's. She stands to greet you, shakes Rosie's hand and then yours. Rosie sits in one of the two chairs opposite her desk just before Sabina Smith says, 'Please, take a seat.'

Rosie says, 'Oops!', leaps to her feet and sits again, all in one motion. The deputy chuckles. You settle into a chair too and brace yourself in the crash position.

'Well, I have to say that was a very impressive letter, young woman.'

Ah, you think, *she's using one of those positive-negative-positive strategies. Start off with something nice, then deliver the bad news, then end with something warm and effusive.*

'Full of commitment and passion,' she continues. 'You're exactly the kind of girl we want at Mount Karver.'

Huh? You wonder if it's a trick. But it's not.

'Thank you!' says Rosie. She turns and beams at you. You smile back.

'Well that's great news,' you say.

Rosie chats happily with Sabina Smith about starting dates and extracurricular activities. At the end of the meeting the deputy opens the door for you and you file out.

'Your limp has almost gone, Mr O'Dell. It's barely discernible at all,' she says.

This surprises you because:

(a) you weren't aware that you were limping anymore, and

(b) you weren't aware that Sabina Smith had been tracking the progress of your limp.

On the way home Rosie hits her phone, texting everyone she's ever met in her entire life. You swing by Macca's for celebratory chocolate thickshakes, half expecting your trusty physician, Doctor David Wilson, to stride disapprovingly through the doors and whip the beverage from your chubby hands. You've been avoiding mirrors lately but you know if you looked you'd find yourself doing an alarmingly accurate impersonation of an over-stuffed sausage.

A girl in a McDonald's cap stands on the table of the booth next to you, hanging tinsel from the ceiling.

'Bit early for Christmas decorations,' you comment to no one in particular.

By way of reply, Rosie lets rip with a mighty burp and adds, 'It's almost December, old man. Get with the program.'

The girl in the McDonald's cap titters.

29

Before your lunch with Rat-tat-tat, you place a phone call that you have been meaning to make for some time. You call Maxx and tell him that you are no longer writing your book on the decline of Australian cinema. You haven't abandoned the idea altogether but you are putting the project on ice. Maxx doesn't even pretend to be surprised. He says he hasn't been in touch because he didn't want to guilt you into writing something you weren't ready to write.

This last part is a fib because you know via a mutual friend that Maxx has been in despair, drinking heavily and showing up intermittently to his ever-shrinking office. Maxx hasn't been in touch because the last thing he needs is another book he can't sell. Most forms of old-school publishing are spiralling down the toilet while Maxx, like every other publisher in the known universe, scrambles to harness the power of the mighty internet to flog his stories. Maxx asks you whether you have any soft porn narratives for the mature female market up your sleeve. You both laugh the same hearty-but-hollow laugh.

You tell Maxx in what you hope is an unpatronising tone that you know times are tough and that you will do your best to return the book advance as soon as you can. Maxx, bless him, screeches, 'Oh don't be so bloody ridiculous, darling!' You're relieved he refuses because, although you feel it's the right thing to do, you have no way of repaying him. 'What are you going to do? he adds. 'Rob a bank?'

You hang up and offer up a brief prayer of thanks that Maxx has graciously released you without fuss. You feel so relieved, you sit down and tell Egg about it. Egg listens intently, occasionally licking your hand. Then you sneak into the bathroom where you wash your licked hands (surreptitiously so as not to offend Egg) and head out to lunch with Rat-tat-tat.

Someone or something has been most unkind to Rat-tat-tat since you saw him last. The man sitting before you is very different from the confident, shiny creature you met a few months back. Today he has dark bags under his haunted eyes and, no longer too busy and important to cater to the pedestrian demands of traditional syntax, he even deigns to employ the occasional pronoun.

Almost as soon as he sits down he launches into a list of woes about the *Herald*. Plummeting circulation. Cutbacks and redundancies. He is in the middle of telling you that no job is safe when his phone rings and he excuses himself to the balcony of the restaurant. You watch his silhouette pace against the blown-out backdrop of the sun-kissed city and think, *Gawd I hope he's not asking me if I know of any jobs.* For a frightening moment this makes complete sense. *Why would he be spending money on you in a fancy restaurant if he didn't want something from you?*

You look around. This is indeed a fancy restaurant. The other impeccably dressed patrons belong to economic strata high above yours. The minimalist, hand-crafted blonde wood furnishings, the five-o'clock-shadowed waiters in crisp white aprons, the Scandinavian cutlery—all tell you that a lot is at stake here for Rat-tat-tat. Ditto the wine list.

Holy fuck, the wine list! You can buy a bottle of wine here for seven thousand dollars!

When he returns to the table you restrain yourself from blurting, 'What do you want?' which is lucky because Rat-tat-tat tells you anyway. Louisa Orban, his star reviewer, is going on maternity leave. It will only be for one year, but he'd like you to replace her.

'Me?'

'Yes,' he says, adding, 'Big workload these days, what with all the online content as well.'

You order your face to arrange itself in a calm and dignified manner.

Do not grin like an idiot.

Do not grin like an idiot.

Do not grin like an idiot.

'Also, I'm thinking it might be time to add a little yin to Lou's yang,' he says with no acknowledgement that he is quoting you from your previous meeting.

'And the…um…?'

'Salary? Same as before, I'm afraid things are pretty tight.'

You order yourself not to leap, weep or hug anyone.

Do not shout yippee.

Do not shout yippee.

214

Do not shout yippee.

'Can I think about it and get back to you?' you ask as if you were a grown-up.

'Please don't make me beg, Michael.'

'Pardon?'

'There's a lot riding on this for me. Pete [*the editor-in-chief*] isn't happy with the arts supplement. My neck is on the line. They want you back. I need to get you back.'

There's a lot that's surprising about this admission:

(a) the frankness about his fragile position,

(b) the insertion of all appropriate pronouns, and

(c) you thought Pete hated you.

You can see the poor guy needs a break just as much as you do. 'When do you want me to start?' you say.

Which is the same question that Wendy asks when you call her from the car to tell her you have a job. 'A month,' you say, and she says, 'Well done, my darling, well done.'

Wendy puts water on to cook some celebration pasta and joins you and Declan in the living room where you are watching television. She hands you a glass of chilled white wine and you clink, holding each other's gaze. This is a custom you acquired on a holiday in Italy before you had children. You can't remember the consequences of not holding each other's gaze while clinking but you remember they're not good.

Lowering herself into one of her shabby-chic cane chairs, Wendy inadvertently sits on the remote control and changes the channel. Instantly realising what she has done, she remedies the situation with the push of a button. A howl of protest from Declan transforms into a woo-hoo of joy.

If only it were always that simple.

Egg, who has been curled up asleep, gets to his feet, shakes himself down and rushes to the window, madly wagging his tail. Moments later he moves to the door as Rosie bursts in with the news that Eva Pessites is definitely going to Mount Karver next year.

The three of you express your horror in unison. Declan even turns off the telly. Rosie says she's okay, that she's talked it through with Eva and she thinks it might work out.

'You talked it through with Eva?' says Wendy, voicing the collective astonishment.

Rosie tells you about overhearing a group of Eva's friends talk in the locker room about Eva going to 'Special K' (Mount Karver). It's the last week of school and there's an unusual air of camaraderie leading up to the Christmas holidays, so Rosie felt emboldened to ask these friends to ask Eva if she would be open to discussing their predicament. During recess, word came back via Maddie Peacock's younger sister, Milly (who is mates with Eva's cousin, Claudia), that Eva was open to dialogue.

Between science and modern history, Rosie saw Eva in the corridor and Eva nodded at her. After a brief discussion, they agreed to meet in the library at lunchtime.

The library at Boomerang occupies the old dormitory wing that once housed the nuns who lived and taught there. Up until the 1960s nuns represented the majority of the teaching staff although today only one ancient nun, Sister

Anastasia, lingers in the art department. At some point during the nineties, the sisters' dormitory was converted into a state-of-the-art library. The stained-glass windows remain preserved in their neo-gothic stone arches, pouring ecclesiastical light over such subversive atheists as Anton Chekhov, George Eliot and Arthur C. Clarke.

As well as the books, heretical and otherwise, there are also elegant pods made from white moulded plastic, designed to house the latest computer technology. It is here that Rosie comes when the lunch bell rings. She waits seven minutes before Eva walks through the door and pauses to look around the library. Rosie stands so that Eva can see her. Eva makes her way over and sits in the pod opposite Rosie without exchanging a word. Once they sit, they cannot see each other but begin to communicate by typing, messaging back and forth on the library's computer network.

Rosie types *We don't have to be friends but we don't have to be enemies either.*

Eva types *Agreed.*

Rosie types *Just because we don't like each other doesn't mean we can't be cool when we see each other at Special K.*

Eva types *Agreed.*

Rosie types *This feud thing is lame. Let's drop it and go our separate ways.*

Eva types *Agreed.* And then she adds *Also we don't talk about each other behind each other's backs.*

Rosie types *Agreed. Especially at Special K.*

Eva types *Agreed.*

Mrs Millington emerges from 440-448 to see Rose O'Dell

shaking hands with Eva Pessites. She is so surprised that she almost drops *Les Ravels sur la plage*, a charming story about the Ravel family's day at the beach that she intends to read to her Year 8 French class. Eva leaves and Mrs Millington makes a beeline to Rosie to find out what on earth that was all about.

Rosie tells Mrs Millington about the truce she and Eva have just declared and Mrs Millington gives her a hug. She tells Rosie how impressed she is by her maturity, and her innovative methodology. 'And I'll tell you this for nothing, Rose: You're going to make a spectacular adult.'

As your daughter tells you this, you look over at Wendy and she's wearing the same expression that always transformed your mother's face in moments of extreme maternal pride: she looks like she's going to crow.

And you want to crow with her.

Then Declan says, 'She's right, Rosie. You are spectacular,' and the moment becomes as perfect as a moment can get. You mentally high-five your wife. You may be a fuck-up but this is one area you have not fucked up. *What are you thinking? Sweep this thought out of your mind! You are inappropriately gloating about your children. The universe will hear you and find you and beat you with a big humility stick.*

Ah, your old friend the Universe.

Fuck you, Universe, I'm going to gloat and delight and dance on the inside. I might just dance on the outside as well.

There is a hissing sound from the kitchen as the pasta water boils over onto the gas cooktop.

'Oh shit, the water!' cries Wendy.

She shoots to her feet and rushes into the kitchen.

30

Christmas draws near and tension in the household rises as you wait for Declan's examination results. The day before they are due, news comes that the education department's computer is in catastrophic meltdown and the results won't be available until January. Declan is frustrated and Wendy is annoyed on his behalf, but you point out that this could be a good thing; at least you won't be managing disappointments over Christmas.

'How do you know there'll be disappointments?' says Wendy. 'He might do okay.' Instead of submitting to your default pessimism, you think, *God, he might do okay. That is a possibility.*

Christmas Day is spent at Ingrid's where she and Tess take the opportunity to tell you that you're looking *so much better* with such overworked spontaneity that you know they've rehearsed it. You know that you are not looking *so much better*, but your weight seems to have reached a plateau; you may have even lost a kilo or two. Occasionally you've overheard Wendy on the phone, voice lowered, discussing your 'progress' with Ingrid or Tess. They have been vigilant guardians, your big sisters. You are about to thank them for this, as you are clearing the table for dessert, when Tess burns the lemon meringue pie and Ingrid tsks. Tess demands to know why Ingrid is tsking. Ingrid asks Tess if she thinks it was wise to leave the pie till the last minute. In a flash things go from pudding to poop and you decide to save your *thank-yous* for another time.

In the new year, you plan to get your book in order. Before you start back at the *Herald*, you want to make sure that there is a clear outline and a useful breakdown of the contents for each chapter in case you ever return to it. One morning after breakfast, you force yourself into the study and close the door. You start by forming a plan of attack.

Step 1: turn on the computer.

You turn on the computer and notice that the screen is dirty and the keyboard could do with a wipe down. You pause to consider whether this is a legitimate concern or a delay tactic. You decide that pausing to consider this is actually a delay tactic so you launch into action. You go and find Wendy and ask her where she has put those industrial wipe things that you use to clean keyboards.

Wendy leads you back into the study and opens the drawer directly in front of where you have been sitting. She retrieves the industrial wipes and refrains from pointing out that the industrial wipes are where they always are: right in front you. You clean the screen with great diligence and wipe carefully around the letters on the keyboard. *My gosh, they're filthy!* You hold the keyboard up to the light and decide they need a second clean.

Once your computer is shipshape and sparkling, you begin work. Well, you would begin work only you look out the window and see the Volvo. *How long has that car been so dirty? My God that car is a disgrace!* You roll back your chair, spring to your feet and stride purposefully into the laundry where you fill a bucket with warm soapy water. You rummage under the laundry sink, looking for the chamois. It's not there. You call out to Wendy and ask if she knows where the chamois is.

Wendy appears at the laundry door and asks what you are doing. You don't answer, 'I'm washing the car,' because you know that's not what she means.

'I thought you were fixing up your book.'

'That car is filthy,' you offer by way of defence.

'Yeah, and I'm about to drive it to my office. If you're looking for some work-avoidance activity, you could run a load of washing.'

She kisses you on the cheek and heads off to her office. You pour the soapy water down the laundry sink and put a pile of dirty clothes into the washing machine. There's enough powder to do this single load but that's all. *Maybe you should walk up to the shops and buy some more?* You catch your reflection in the round window of the clothes dryer that hangs

221

above the washer. You know perfectly well what you are doing and it's time to surrender.

Defeated, you return to the study and your gleaming computer. You read over what you have written previously and begin to type out a plan of how to proceed. Now that you have committed to placing the project in metaphoric mothballs, the ideas flow and the writing unfolds as if you are channelling someone who knows what they are talking about.

You feel a presence behind you and turn to discover your son hovering at the study door.

'Sorry to interrupt...'

'Come in, sit!' you say enthusiastically.

'I got my marks back for my film; I got an A-plus.'

'Wow. An A-plus! Well done, that's great!'

'Thanks.'

'You must be so pleased!'

'I am, I am...'

'Well, I'm not surprised. You did a brilliant job.'

'Thanks, Dad...'

Just when you are working well, when you no longer require a distraction, one has arrived. You are tempted to turn back to your computer and resume typing but you don't because you have the feeling there is something else your son wants to tell you. Or something he doesn't want to tell you but feels he must. You don't push it. You smile and nod, holding his gaze until he says, 'So that's the good news.'

Uh-huh.

Weirdly, you don't panic. Your palms go sweaty but your heart does not race and you do not have to fight the urge to

222

hide under your desk. Declan sits in the broken office chair that Wendy normally uses. He picks at the black gaffer tape binding the torn vinyl cover to the seat.

'Remember the pencil case and the drugs thing?'

You nod again.

'I was in on it…James was going to give me ten per cent of whatever he made. That's why I was minding them.'

Of course. Of course that's what was happening. Anyone other than you with your unique head-in-the-sand approach to parenting would have seen it. But now you must deal with it. He has come to you and you alone. Wendy is not here. Deal with it like a proper father.

'Thank you for telling me. I appreciate you telling me the truth.'

He looks at you. *There needs to be more.* You don't want to say, 'I'm very disappointed in you,' because that feels so predictable but the fact remains that you are disappointed so you say—

'I'm very disappointed in you.' You shake your head. 'I thought, I know, that you know better.'

'I know. It was…dumb.'

'And wrong. Very wrong. That's the main thing. It's wrong to sell drugs to vulnerable kids. Kids who may get addicted, kids who may die from their addiction. You could have been responsible for someone's death.'

Declan looks at you, horrified. *Good. Be afraid, be very afraid.* You can see he is about to cry. 'Indirectly responsible but responsible nonetheless,' you say. 'Take a deep breath.'

Declan takes a deep breath. 'I'm sorry,' he says.

'Why are you telling me this now? Has something come up about it?'

'No, I was just thinking about it. I wanted you to know is all.'

'Well I appreciate that, I really do. It takes guts to admit something like that.'

He smiles through his frown and nods his gratitude for this small concession. Now it is your turn to come clean.

'I took them,' you say.

'What?'

'The drugs. I found them in your room and I threw them out.'

You can see him wondering whether to go on the offensive or not. 'Why didn't you tell me?'

'I just did.'

Clever answer but not a good one. You know you should have told him before this but the truth is that you were frozen in the headlights of your own inaction. You let the opportunity pass and then you couldn't think how or when to say what you needed to say. It became harder to raise the matter and easier to let it drop. You were able to do this by telling yourself you had more important things to deal with.

Perhaps you did. Perhaps you didn't.

You watch your son crossing a moral tightrope, balancing up who should have told what to whom and when. You don't want him to detour into an argument about your own ethical turpitude, not because you are afraid of the fight, but because he deserves better. He has had the courage to raise this transgression when it could just as easily have been discarded in

224

a quiet corner. He deserves this to be about him, not you. So you take back control by asking—

'What on earth possessed you to do something like that in the first place?'

He shrugs. 'I dunno…James asked me to.'

This is not a very good answer either but you have no doubt it is a truthful one. You recall Wendy and Mel riffing about the insanity of adolescent peer pressure. There's no point in saying, 'Well if James jumped off a thirty-storey building, would you jump off too?' because the amazing answer is that, yes, he would jump. At this age, he would do anything to be like his friends.

You wonder what to do about the issue of punishment. He's obviously contrite and perhaps being beaten black and blue by his good mate James (*note to self: scowl nastily at James next time he breezes through with a 'Hey Mr O'*) is punishment enough, but still you tell him that you will discuss the matter with his mother when she comes home.

'Just assure me that you know it was wrong,' you say. 'That you know this is not the way good men behave.'

'I know it was wrong.'

'Don't do it again. You're better than that.'

'I won't. I promise.'

He doesn't add, as he is entitled to, 'But you were wrong too; you should have told me you had thrown the drugs away.' He does not say this because he appreciates that in the grand scheme of things the withholding of such information is a comparatively minor offence, and because he has a generous spirit, your boy. You stand up, put your arms around him and hug him tight. He mumbles *sorry* again into your shoulder and you let him go.

'I'm glad I told you.'

'I'm glad you told me too.'

On the day the high school examination results finally come out, you wake early. Summer rain is sheeting down and you drag yourself out of bed. Egg greets you as if you have risen from the dead which, for all he knows, you have. A familiar dripping sound leads you down the hall to discover—*rediscover*—a leak in the skylight you had inexpensively installed in the dark dining room when you first moved in. Water drip drip drips into an expanding puddle on the worn pine floorboards. You towel them dry and place a bucket under the drip, only to discover that there is a second drip. Wendy shuffles in, bleary-eyed.

'I thought you fixed that,' she says.

'So did I,' you answer.

Just over a year ago, you pumped enough silicon into the space around the skylight to fill a swimming pool. Now the leak is back, trumpeting its victory over you by demanding not one but two buckets.

'I hope it's not an omen,' you say, all gloom and grumpy doom.

Wendy looks at you hard and shuffles back down the hall to brush her teeth. By the time you join her, the rain has stopped and a small patch of blue has opened in the grey above the bathroom window.

'Well I'll be...It *is* an omen,' says Wendy in a silly

cheesy voice. 'The world has been washed clean.'

The phone rings and you both hear Declan spring out of bed to answer it.

'More miracles,' you add in the same silly voice although it doesn't sound nearly as funny or original when you do it.

And anyway, it's not a miracle. It's no surprise at all. Some of Declan's mates already have their results via the internet. They are calling, texting and facebooking, celebrating or commiserating.

Declan, unusually, has elected to receive his results in hard copy via snail mail. The letter should come today but because she has to leave for work, Wendy encourages Declan to log on and check his results. He says he can't be bothered, which Rosie points out is a big fat lie. Wendy leaves on the promise that Declan will call her as soon as he knows anything. The household busies itself with other tasks but everyone keeps an ear out for the postman, unnecessarily because Egg will go off his head once the red motor scooter is within a three-house radius.

Just after 11am Egg goes off his head and Rosie shoots out the door like a rocket. Declan shouts, 'Hey!' and races after her. He pushes Rosie off the path and she plummets into an azalea, laughing. The postman grins because he has been similarly greeted by other expectant eighteen-year-olds and knows exactly what is at stake here. He hands Declan his letter and says, 'Good luck.'

At that moment, Egg bursts through the unlatched screen door and charges down the path, hackles raised, barking ferociously. Declan tries to dive tackle him but the wretched dog wriggles free. The postman shouts, 'Egg! Sit!' and (rather pathetically) Egg sits, looking guilty. Rosie resurrects herself from the azaleas and grabs Egg by the collar. Declan apologises but the postman says he enjoys it.

'Me and Egg, we have a thing,' he explains.

Rosie and Declan come inside and you get Wendy on the phone and all huddle around the kitchen table for the Reading of the Results. Declan rips the letter open with mock ferocity. As he scans it you all unhelpfully add to the tension by taking turns with single-word questions.

'And?'

'Yes?'

'What?'

'Good?'

Declan finishes reading and hands you the results with a slightly nonplussed look on his face. 'Good,' he says. You read the results to Wendy. They're better than good; they're great. He's hoping to do journalism or law and these marks should get him into either. Wendy asks you to remind him to call his cousin Mel.

You start to plan a special celebration dinner but Declan overhears you and says he'll probably be out. 'Fair enough,' you say, 'we'll do it another time.' Declan calls Mel on his mobile and even Wendy can hear her whoops of delight. You all laugh at Mad Mel's enthusiasm.

All four members of Team O'Dell are laughing at the same thing at the same time. You try to remember the last time this happened but you can't.

31

You are in the backyard with Wendy, excavating the ruins of the vegetable garden that you laid out two seasons ago and promptly abandoned. Making feverish trips to the nursery, you purchased railway sleepers for the borders and filled them with two tons of top quality (organic!) soil that some idiot delivery man almost dumped directly on your driveway before you charged out and stopped him, laying out a tarpaulin to protect the gravel.

You borrowed your neighbour's flat-tyred wheelbarrow and, being the Big Strong Man that you are, ferried the soil from the front to the back garden in no time. Well, not no time, half a day, actually. After your impressive effort, you presented your freshly bulging biceps for Wendy's inspection and she laughed. *Cackled*, some might say. In playful retaliation, you threw a handful of soil at her but this didn't turn out to be the hilarious back-lit romp amongst the daisies that you envisioned when dirt got stuck behind her contact lens and she rushed off to the bathroom, blinded.

Half an hour later Wendy returned with a swollen red eye and silently began to plant enough vegetable seedlings to feed a starving nation. If said nation had been counting on your baby lettuces, carrots, beans, rocket, tomatoes and cauliflowers to mature into edible adulthood, they would indeed have starved because four weeks later you went camping during a heatwave and the whole lot died.

You swore it was Wendy's job to ask the neighbour to do the watering while you were gone. Wendy swore it was yours.

Your current argument revolves around the (evidently drought-resistant) lemon tree. You are bickering about whether to leave it as the centrepiece of the vegetable killing fields (let sleeping dogs lie, you say) when Rosie appears and tells you she has some news.

You both freeze.

'No, no, no. It's not that bad,' Rosie quickly adds. 'It's just a bit...sad, I guess?'

Now she really has your attention.

'Juan and I broke up.'

Wendy peels off the rubber washing-up gloves that she has been using in lieu of proper gardening gloves and goes to hug Rosie.

'Oh darling!' she proclaims but Rosie puts up her hands, cutting the hug off at the pass.

'I'm okay, I'm okay,' she says.

'Are you sure?'

'Absolutely positively. Geez, Mum. Have a panic, why don't you?'

You're reluctant to be the one to ask the obvious question but you say, 'What happened?'

'We had a bit of a fight and he said, "Maybe we should call it quits" and I said, "Maybe we should",' she says with a shrug. 'So we did.'

'So *he* called it off?' you ask, amazed.

'They both did,' counters Wendy defensively.

'No, Juan did really,' says Rosie, 'but that's okay.'

'You seem okay,' says Wendy, sounding slightly surprised.

'Yeah I am okay. I'm…relieved.'

Relieved. It's the same word she used when Juan moved out and you think: *Of course you're relieved, you poor sweetheart. Smarter parents would have put an end to things long before the boy had your name tattooed across his chest.*

You don't give voice to this but you do silently hope that one day when Rosie is lying on a psychiatrist's couch she will forgive you for your lack of vigilance.

Later, when you are watching television, Rosie executes a kind of somersault over the back of the couch and snuggles in between you and Wendy. You both wrap your arms around her and she allows you to cuddle her. You don't get many cuddles these days but this, you note, is a good one.

You feel your luck. First about the hug but then in a cosmic sense: you are part of something far bigger than yourself that travels to your children and to their children and their children and on and on. *Rosie's children.*

Now there's a thought.

Wendy looks over at you, blinking slowly as a way of saying, 'This is bliss.'

You drive around the maze of city fringe laneways, searching for a park. A red car pulls out in front of you and your heart leaps. You accelerate the old Volvo before some zippy little number materialises and nips into the spot, invalidating your claim on it. Quickly *the* spot forms in your mind as *your* spot, but sadly when you get there, it's a No Standing zone. You consider whether to park illegally but you will be here for at least an hour, maybe ninety minutes, because you are visiting your psychiatrist. In that time a parking inspector is bound to come along and while insanity may be mounted as a defence for murder, you're not sure you can offer it up as a defence for illegal parking.

You're wishing you could channel some of Wendy's excellent parking karma, when you do: two small cars pull out across the road, leaving room for one ancient dinosaur-sized Volvo. You execute a U-turn and reverse cleanly into the spot. There is no argy-bargy back and forth. No am-I-close-enough-to-the-kerb? No have-I-left-enough-room-for-the-car-in-front? Just a perfectly realised reverse park. If you were in a parking competition right now, each of the three admiring judges would award you ten out of ten. You lock the car and walk briskly down the street because you're running a little late. Normally you'd be all flustered and sweaty but you're not. Maybe it's because you're a gold-medal-winning parkiologist. Parkographer? Parker?

Soon you're lying on your psychiatrist's couch discussing *Zorba the Greek*. *As you do.* You talk about the part where Zorba's friend's business collapses and he loses everything he has worked for. In response, the guy goes dancing down the beach, rejoicing because he is suddenly stripped back to his bare self. Instead of despair he feels 'a sublime unjustifiable gladness. Not only unjustifiable but contrary to all justification...As if in the hard sombre labyrinth of necessity I had discovered liberty herself playing happily in a corner. And I played with her.'

You wish you felt like that. Doctor Maurice smiles ruefully.

Books and movies in particular, he comments, often present big crises followed by swift resolutions; that is a large part of their appeal. The bridge blows up so the hero stops the train. The children are kidnapped so the heroine recovers them. The dragon threatens the princess so the knight slays it. Obvious problems. Simple solutions. Life, unfortunately, is messier.

You sit in silence for a while.

Sometimes, you think, the only thing to do is *endure*. Sometimes the great act of heroism is simply getting out of bed. For some people on some days that is a stupendous achievement. It's not sexy or epic but it is heroic.

You smile and tell Doctor Maurice how, when the accident first happened, you decided that you had been Called to Adventure, that you were about to embark on a Hero Journey and that the universe would reveal Truths to you. He laughs and asks what you have learned.

'The message is, there is no message,' you say. 'Or maybe

there is a message but it's too soppy to repeat.'

'Fair enough.'

At the end of the session Doctor Maurice suggests that you begin cutting down on your antidepressants: instead of two pills, one and three-quarters. You say, yes, you're ready. You hope your weight loss will improve once you stop with the high dosages; your GP says if you don't stop eating, you're going to explode. Doctor Maurice chuckles. 'You look like you've lost a little to me.'

'I think I have,' you say.

He walks you to the door.

'It's strange.'

'What?' he asks.

'You know everything about me and I know nothing about you.'

'Yeah, I often think that too!' calls Em, eavesdropping from the reception desk.

She's dyed her hair bright pink.

32

At the one-year anniversary of being run over by Frannie Prager's blue sedan, you are rummaging under the house looking for the long pole with the pruning shears on the end that were left suspended under the floor joists by the previous owners. They are not in the usual spot so you grab a torch from the hall cupboard and move deeper into the gloom. Your light beam catches a pair of crutches that you realise are *your* crutches from the accident. This surprises you because you thought someone had taken them back to the hospital. You remember that they were merely loaned to you by the emergency department. You drag them into the daylight to discover that except for a fine layer of dust they're in perfect condition.

Up in the kitchen you wipe them down with the

washing-up cloth. Wendy doesn't like the washing-up cloth used for anything other than washing-up but Wendy's not here. You rinse the washing-up cloth thoroughly (erasing all signs of domestic disobedience) and think *No time like the present* so you take the crutches down to the car and drive them back to the hospital.

Walking up the ramp of the emergency department you rehearse an explanation.

'Sorry, I thought someone had returned them.'

No, take responsibility for them yourself.

'Sorry, I forgot they were under the house.'

No, you didn't know they were under the house; stop taking blame for mistakes you didn't make.

'Look what I found under my house!'

No, you should show some repentance for keeping them out of action for six months longer than necessary. Actually, why should you? It's not as if you meant to keep them out of action. Why not simply remain anonymous?

'Look what I found in the car park! Someone must have left them there.'

No, why would you compound the wrong by lying about it as well?

You walk through the plastic swing door at the top of the ramp to discover the emergency department fragrant with sweat, fear and hospital-grade disinfectant. The waiting room overflows with patients; some even lie on the floor. It's hard to tell who is sick and who is there to support the sick. The nurses at the triage station are run off their feet.

Your why-I-haven't-returned-my-crutches alibi suddenly

seems insignificant. Gently you lean the crutches against a pillar and, without a word of explanation to anyone, leave. It's neither heroic nor courageous but you have returned the crutches to their rightful place.

On the way home you find yourself cruising down a shady avenue lined with high-walled mansions and realise that you are approaching the pedestrian crossing where you were run down by the blue sedan. You make sure no one is waiting to cross because it would be appropriately Kafkaesque for you to run someone over here exactly a year to the day after you were run over. In your version of the story you would run over the woman who ran you over, Frannie Prager, and the attending officer would be Constable Lance Johnstone.

Fortunately the street is empty and you drive over the crossing without incident.

Then, on a whim, you pull over and walk back to the scene of the crime. You imagine yourself on the other side of the road and see yourself walking across, connecting with the blue car, sliding up the hood, smashing the windscreen, catapulting through the air and landing in the gutter, a vivid replay with anatomically correct detailing like one of those awful drive-carefully ads you see on TV.

All you think is: *so that happened.*

You explore the quiet corners of your head or your heart or your gut or wherever suppressed feelings hide but nothing emerges.

Just: *so that happened.*

This seems way too normal a response for someone as catastrophically inclined as yourself. You cross the crossing.

You stand there looking, waiting. A woman appears at her front gate and pretends to be sorting through her mail rather than assessing your potential as a thief/rapist/vandal/graffitist.

It occurs to you that this could be the very same lady who placed a blanket over you or patted your back a year ago today. You decide to go over and introduce yourself and thank her for her kindness. You are about to cross back when you see a silver Jaguar coming. It slows but you wave it past, and by the time it has gone, so has the woman.

Probably wasn't her anyway. So you return to the car and drive home.

The gravel of your driveway crunches comfortingly under your tyres. The French doors of the converted garage are open and Declan is inside, waxing his surfboard. He comes to greet you.

'Hi Fatty,' he says.

'Shut up,' you grin back as you hoist yourself out of the old Volvo.

Your son looks up and you follow his gaze into the achingly blue sky. It is a glorious late summer's day. You feel the warm air ebb around you.

'How about a walk?' you ask even though you know the offer will be declined.

'Sure,' he says.

You go inside and change your shoes while Declan puts his surfboard back in its silvery plastic cover and locks it in the room where Juan was once ensconced.

'Do you miss him?' he asks when you return in the battered runners that you have not run in for exactly one year.

'Who?' you ask.

'Juan.'

'Oh. No, not really. Do you?'

'Nah. I wish him well, but.'

At the end of the driveway you usually turn right towards the dip in the road that eventually leads to the dead end where suburbia meets the bush. But Declan steers left and leads you up the hill, across the main road, and back down a tree-lined avenue of modest timber cottages. Here and there a house has been bulldozed and replaced by a brick McMansion, one of those neo-Federation confections with a living room and a family room and a rumpus room and a media room and a conservatory, designed so that no member of the resident family need ever cross paths with any other member.

'You haven't been walking much lately,' says Declan.

'Cars still freak me out a bit,' you confess. As if to prove the potential danger, a yellow Volkswagen Beetle tears around the corner, forcing you off the road and onto the verge.

'You should come surfing with me.'

You laugh at his joke.

'I'm *serious*.'

'I'm too old.'

'Not for a long board. There's plenty of old blokes out there on long boards.'

'Yeah but I'll bet they've been doing it since they were kids.'

'Not all of them. It's not that hard once you learn the basics. Then it's just practice and persistence.'

You look at your son, touched that he is trying to involve

you in his favourite sport. You don't want to hurt his feelings so you say, 'Well thank you. I'll give it some thought.'

'*And* there are no cars out there in the surf,' he adds as a kind of incentive.

'Yeah, but there are sharks.'

'Which is why I'm a very fast paddler,' he says. 'Come on.' Declan heads down a battleaxe driveway.

'Where are you going? This is someone's house.'

'No it's not, it's a fire trail.'

You have lived in this suburb almost your entire life and you have passed this long strip of basalt gravel thousands of times. But this is the first time you walk down it. You follow your son and find yourself in a part of the bush that you never knew existed.

You arrive in a clearing behind a group of houses. A black ring of grass bespeaks a once-mighty, probably-communal, certainly-illegal bonfire. You imagine the neighbours gathering here, dragging fallen logs from the bordering bushland and adding their own building offcuts to create a great mound of wood. Night falls and the man from number 42 splashes his mower fuel over the timber mountain. Mothers withdraw their children to a safe distance. A match strikes and—*whoosh*—the fire is away! Young and old watch mesmerised as the flames leap and roar. Sparks spiral magically into the dark sky.

'Oi. This way,' says Declan, stirring you from your reverie.

Beyond the clearing an old wooden bridge spans a tinkling creek. Declan leads you across, following the fire trail again. The track is muddy in parts, lined with wattle and glossy shrubs with dark green leaves. Sydney blue gums and angophora with almost-human limbs tower tall as skyscrapers above your head. Their vast canopies rustle in the gentlest of breezes.

The word *zephyr* pops into your head.

The world smells warm and damp and at irregular intervals the perfume of eucalypt flowers assaults your senses. You come to a sandstone ledge jutting over the creek where it swells into a small pool. It reminds you of suicide rock and you blush at your foolishness. Declan sits and you sit next to him. He drapes his arm casually across your shoulder and those damn tears spring to your eyes once again. Fortunately your son is looking down into the water that mirrors the green canopy and sky above.

You blink back the tears without him noticing.

He lies back and folds his hands behind his head, looking up through the trees to bits of the blue beyond. You remain sitting, staring into the reflection on the water's surface and realise that you and your son are looking at the same thing.

Not a word passes between you. In the silence you become dimly aware of a distant hum. Slowly the sound builds in your consciousness and you wonder where it is coming from. Then a whiff of eucalypt reminds you that way, way above your head the trees are flowering; they will be filled with millions of bees occupied with their harvesting. You can't see them. You can barely hear them. But you know they are there.

And now you are aware of something else. A mighty river flowing below you. And above you. And all around you.

Some people never know this river. Others are destined

to feel only the occasional splash. Others dive in and out but still don't feel enough of it. But you, you are in the river, swept along in the torrent, sometimes floating, sometimes drowning, spluttering, flailing but always soaked in it.

You are an unremarkable man living an unremarkable life except for this single thing: you love and are splendidly loved. You will never paint a masterpiece or engineer a great bridge or leave any lasting monument to yourself. But you have been swept into the river of love and you know how to swim there and you are teaching your children how to swim as your parents taught you and your children will teach theirs and on it will go.

This is your legacy, your luck, your glory and your magnificence.

You lie back on the hard ground next to your son. You know it can't be true but you feel like you are levitating.

Acknowledgments

I'd like to thank Margaret Connolly for her considered counsel and for believing that this small offering might be something worth publishing. I'd like to thank Michael Heyward for agreeing with her and for his great skill and enthusiasm, both as publisher and editor. Along with Anne Beilby, he has also been a wonderful promoter of this novel internationally. Thanks to my other editor, Mandy Brett, for her attentiveness, humour, kindness and rigour, Chong Weng Ho for his brilliant cover and for summarising my book so succinctly to me ('middle-class loser makes good'), Kirsty Wilson and Shalini Kunahlan, Michelle Calligaro, Imogen Stubbs, the perfectly named Natalie Book, and publicist extraordinaire Jane Novak. The thing that shines about you people is your genuine love of books. You are inspirational. Thank you.

Thanks also to Phil Rich, Richard Mortlock, Kim Maine, Susan Vass, Joanna Weinberg and Menno Meyjes for their assistance and guidance. And for being there.

Finally, thank you to the large, rambling assortment of oddments that make up my family over three continents and two hemispheres. I'd especially like to thank my sisters, Trish Mair and Helen Bateman, my wife, Klay, to whom this book is dedicated and without whom it would not exist, my wondrous children, Louis and Gina, the fortuitously addended Nell, and last but not least delightful, delovely Delilah Rose Lamprell, who makes everything brand new again.

MARK LAMPRELL has worked in film and television for many years. He co-wrote the film *Babe: Pig in the City* and wrote and directed the award-winning feature *My Mother Frank*. His most recent project is the movie musical *Goddess*, which he co-wrote and directed. *The Full Ridiculous* is his first novel.